RUBY FIRE

— · —

THE WITCH BROTHER SAGA, BOOK THREE

ADAM J. RIDLEY

BLAKE ALLWOOD PUBLISHING

Printed in the United States of America

Box Elder, SD

First Printing: September 2022

Blake Allwood Publishing

Ebook ISBN: 978-1-956727-32-6

Paperback ISBN: 978-1-956727-33-3

Library of Congress Control Number: 2022914082

— · —

CONTENT WARNINGS

Homophobia
Controlling Parents
Explicit Sex Scenes
Child Abuse
Violence

Join Blake's email list to get advance notice of new books and receive his occasional newsletter:

www.blakeallwood.com

MM Romance
By Blake Allwood

Transitions Series
Aiden Inspired
Suzie Empowered (MF Romance)
Bobby Transformed

Chance Series
Love By Chance
Another Chance With Love
Taking A Chance For Love

Romantic Series
Romantic Renovations (1)
Romantic Rescue (2)
Romantic Recon (3)

Melody Series
Melody of the Heart
Melody of the Snow

Road to Rocktoberfest Anthology
Changing His Tune - 2022

Coming Home Series (2023)
A Long Way Home
Family Home
Down Home
…and many more

Novellas
Tenacious
Moon's Place

Romantic Fantasy
By Adam J. Ridley

Big Bend Series
Love's Legacy (1)
Love's Heirloom (2)
Love's Bequest (3)

The Witch Brothers Series
Emerald Earth
Diamond Air
Ruby Fire
Sapphire Water

Acknowledgments

Special thanks to the following amazing people who helped me get this book finished and into your hands.

Jo Bird: Editor
Renee Mizar: Editor
Alma Alexander: Editor
Ann Attwood: Proofreader

And of course, a big thank you to my husband who puts up with my endless stories and handles the formatting and final publishing of all my books.

ONE

PROLOGUE

KYLE

"A RE YOU PACKED?" EARL, my doctorial counterpart, asked.

"Well, of course, I'm not packed. Why would I pack?"

"'Cause Dr. Fagan fired you?"

"Yeah, he fires me all the time. What else is new? Earl, I need to see the latest readings for expansion."

"Kyle!"

I turned to see my university professor and mentor, not to mention one of the world's leading volcanologists, walk into the room.

"Dr. Fagan, I was just going over the latest measurements."

The older man stopped in front of me, put his hand on my shoulder, and said, "No, son. You're going home. You disobeyed my orders, again. You could've been seriously hurt, or worse, you could've put other people's safety in jeopardy."

"It had to be done. The sensor was essential for our..."

"The sensor wasn't worth your life, or anyone else's."

I sighed. "Okay, I've learned my lesson. I'll be more careful next time."

Both Earl and Dr. Fagan chuckled. Apparently, they knew as well as I did that was a lie.

"That's unlikely. Regardless, I've already told Dr. Agnes you're headed back to Eugene and the U of O."

"Seriously? I'm named in the grant. You can't just force me back to Oregon."

"You are named as a research assistant and Ph.D. student. Your job is done with regard to the grant." Dr. Fagan's smile never left his face. How was he always so damned chipper? "Besides, I'm sure Popocatépetl will continue erupting without you."

I decided to nod and just walk out. This wasn't the first time I'd violated one of Dr. Fagan's endless rules, and probably wouldn't be the last. Not that I was reckless, I just... well, I just did things a little differently. In any case, I wasn't going to leave the mountain. I had too much at stake. I'd fought my way up through a very cliquish group of graduate students to get this opportunity, and wasn't about to give it up. I was so close to earning my Ph.D. and, considering my dissertation was almost entirely based around Mexico's Popocatépetl volcano, it only made sense for me to stay.

Forget the fact that Dr. Agnes had told me I needed to come back to the states, or rather, I needed to sit down and finish writing my dissertation. I had a real-live active volcano on my hands, and not just any volcano. The stately cone-shaped beauty of Popocatépetl herself was practically calling to me! Even the promise of *finally* finishing graduate school wasn't lure enough to return to campus anytime soon.

When I got back to the foot of the mountain, I flopped onto my small cot, frustrated, but determined. I was just starting to drift off when I saw her.

"Grandma?" I asked out loud, and sat up to get a better look. She smiled at me.

"You're needed at home!" she said, and I shook my head.

"Grandma, why are you here?"

"Like I said, you're needed at home."

"I can't just go home. I have a job to do. Popocatépetl could erupt any day now!"

The wisps of smoke making up Grandma's body began to sway, and I blinked. "Hey, you're dead," I said like an idiot.

"You always were the bright one. If I'm not mistaken, Kyle, you no longer have a job here, or did I not hear correctly?"

That annoyed me. I'd lived with my grandmother from my teen years onward, after my parents kicked my brothers and me out of the house, because we all came out as gay. Well, they came out as gay, I came out as bisexual. Our lives were thrown into chaos for a while after that, never mind I was only just figuring out my sexuality at the time. But, all these years later, it was water under a bridge I never dared cross. As far as I was concerned, dwelling on the past was a waste of time and energy better spent elsewhere... like on an active volcano about to blow.

The only good thing to come out of that childhood trauma—as one of my school counselors had called it—was moving in with the solid rock of a loving and quirky woman that was our grandmother. I'd always been intensely fond of her, and her death had felt like a gut-punch to the only stable and constant aspect of my life.

I shook off the thought and focused back on Grandma, who true to form—despite not having an actual form in this world any longer—was giving me shit. Just as I was about to contradict her about my questionable job status, though, a dark shadow moved behind her. She looked back at it quickly and then glanced at me, concern etched on her face. And was that... fear?

Grandma had never been afraid of anything in this life, other than—as she told me many times—her three beloved grandsons living lonely lives, never finding true happiness. It was at that moment I knew the dark shadow had to represent the curse Dad had cast upon us as kids. That wicked damning to never know the love of another man, was the only possible thing to cause Grandma such distress from beyond the veil.

"Things are getting dangerous here, Kyle." She looked at the darkness and her scowl deepened. "Your father's cantation has fought both of your brothers. They won, love triumphed for them, but I'm sorry, it's now your time. You need to come home if I'm to protect you."

"I can't just go, Grandma..." I started to say, when the cursed cantation lunged for me.

I held my hands up to prevent the darkness from devouring me, and noticed Grandma shift out of focus, swirl in what appeared to be some sort of tornado, and rush toward me. She reached me before the cantation did, but I was caught up in her whirlwind.

"Kyle? Hey, Kyle, wake up!"

"Lance?" I asked, confused. Why was Lance in Puebla, Mexico?

"Kyle, wake up!" he demanded, and I finally opened my eyes.

The first thing I noticed was Lance standing over me, wearing a robe of all things. The second thing I noticed was the circle of people, which included Grandma's former roommate Drew Andreassen, surrounding us... and all but Lance standing entirely in the buff.

Then, I felt the cold stone against my skin, and realized that I, too, was stark naked and lying on an altar in the middle of Grandma's garden. I was back in Chemeketa? What about Popocatépetl?

"What the fuck? What happened?" Several of the women around us chuckled. "Lance? Did you summon me by magic?" I asked, confused since my eldest brother had been a skeptic. He'd spent years denying our abilities even existed, let alone used them.

He shook his head and laughed. "You know I wouldn't have a clue how to do that. You were the one Grandma taught all that magic stuff to." He looked me over and laughed harder. "Dude, you're kinda naked. Why don't you go with Drew and get dressed? You're about his size. We can discuss the way you got here when you stop giving these folks a peep show."

"Shit, yeah," I said, looking down at my naked form again once I stood up. It was either that, or risk gawking at the naked elders around us, and, well, I could already feel a blush creeping up my neck as I tried with only mild success to cover myself with my hands.

I mean, this wasn't the first time I'd been naked in front of a coven of witches. Truth be known, it wasn't the first time I'd been teleported either, although, up until now, I'd only gone from one part of my grandmother's conjuring circle to another.

What was beyond the realm of my already-strange normal was the dream of my grandmother. Now that I thought about it, given her insistence on my returning here, I knew it was she who'd sent me home.

Lance, Drew, and I didn't do much talking that night, even after everyone else had gone home. Teleporting took a lot out of a person, and I only had enough energy left to drag myself to my old bedroom to sleep.

Two

Conley

MY MOTHER WRAPPED THE warm blanket around my shoulders. "You should try not to anger the dragons while you are… well, just try not to speak," she said, and, of course, I wanted to cross my eyes and say something smart.

I'd always had a smart mouth, and it often got me in trouble, but the dragons had all been restless lately. Each of the three volcanoes that surrounded our community were called "dragons" because they breathed fire, and were as finicky as you'd imagine a real dragon would be.

"I'll behave, Mama," I said. "I'd avoid the quest altogether, except the old man said I had to go."

"That old man is your father and the leader of our village. The fact you have resisted doing your vision quest is beyond anyone's understanding, Conley. Most young people are chomping at the bit to go."

It was an old argument, and it did no good for me to explain to my parents again that I didn't want to go, because of the ominous feeling I got every time I considered it. The dragons – in actual dragon form, not as mountains like they were in reality – had visited me in dreams all my life. They'd told me themselves not to go on my quest until I was ready. If only they would tell that to my parents too.

"You must be ready to take up the mantle of leadership, and it will weigh heavily on you, Conley Bolcan."

Being well into adulthood, I was no longer able to avoid it. Only one other person in the history of Dóiteán who'd waited in making their vision quest with the dragons had been my great-great-grandmother.

She'd refused to go until she was twenty-three. When she delayed, the dragon began to erupt in an area south of what is now called Lassen National Park in the other world. The year was nineteen hundred and fourteen, and she'd wanted to avoid being the leader of the community. She was determined to return to the parallel dimension from which our ancestors had left. *Intrigued by the stories of large cities and pretty dresses*, that was how my father had told the story.

In the end, she'd given in and gone on the quest, and had returned to become the community's leader—one of the most renowned and revered, at that. As much as her story inspired and intrigued me, I didn't want to repeat her experiences. I didn't have any particular interest in seeing the outside world. As our population had grown, we'd created our own cities, and those who'd migrated to our world said it was better here anyway.

Her mother and my third great-grandmother, Luna Raven, was an Irish immigrant. She'd crossed two oceans, traveling around the continent of the Americas before landing along the Oregon coast. Upon reaching Chemeketa–a village on the other side of the dimension from ours–she'd passed through the cave that linked our worlds and founded our town. No one knew if she named it Dóiteán, which in Gaelic meant fire, because of the volcanoes, or because our community became a haven for fire elementals.

I slipped the blanket off my shoulders, rolling it tight and tying a ribbon around it, binding it to the bottom of my pack. Mama had made sure to pack plenty of food for my journey. All of Dóiteán's young people going on their quest were instructed to spend their first night in a cave that had its own food store, but since I'd decided to wait until the solstice had passed, it was very likely a blizzard could keep me from reaching the cave. The mountains we called the dragons tended to be snowy, especially this time of year. It was more than likely I'd encounter at least one storm up there, so it was best to be prepared; it could make a difference between survival, or never coming back.

I kissed my mother, and sighed when I realized my father had yet to return home. I was sure he was still annoyed by our last argument. So, alone and without saying goodbye to my father, I began the slow trudge along the lane leading up the mountainside. I made it out of the village before I looked up the steep incline of Dragon Dubh—black dragon in Gaelic—which was called Dubh for short. The black dragon was the largest of the three.

In my dreams, it was male and more red than black, but the dark volcanic soil that still showed through the forests and glaciers earned it the name from the first settlers to come here.

We'd lived here for over a century and a half, appeasing, or rather, appealing to the dragons to maintain their tempers, and not erupt in ways that would destroy the land.

Even before Earth's scientists discovered the link between long winters, climate change, and volcanic activity, we, the people of Dóiteán, had known. Now it was our destiny to keep the dragons of the Cascades from being too... obnoxious.

Just as I was thinking about it, the ground rumbled below me. "If I can't be honest, what good am I going to do anyone?" I said out loud, speaking to all three dragons.

From an early age, my relationship with the dragons probably made me too familiar. That was what my father had said anyway. But, so far, they didn't seem to mind that much. Although, I guessed like my father and mother, I knew the dragons would prefer less honesty and more diplomacy. Oh, well, that was never going to be my gift.

Although the dragons had shown themselves to several of my ancestors throughout the years, it'd only been a few times throughout their lifetimes. However, sometime around my sixth birthday, I realized I had a relationship with them that was unlike the other people in our community, including my parents. For me, the dragons had always been more real than merely symbolic.

I climbed the entire day, snow starting to fall slowly and silently around me as I got higher, but not yet a blizzard. I made it to the cave without issues, and when twilight began to fall, I started a fire and began warming up the now frozen food my mother had packed for me.

It was customary to sleep on the mountain for three days. If the dragons had a purpose for you, they would share it during the quest. It was a rite of passage connecting the volcanoes with the people who'd sworn to do their bidding.

It was our destiny to serve the dragons. Not just the three that stood sentinel here, but all volcanoes in the Cascades, as well as those that flowed along what the other world now called the Ring of Fire. As long as we were here and willing to participate, we could predict and manage the worst of the eruptions. As the population on Earth had skyrocketed since Dóiteán was settled, that became even more important.

After finishing my meal, I lay down on the small cot kept in the cave, pulling the woolen blanket around me, and settling in for the evening. Although I knew this was supposed to be an auspicious time, I didn't do much ceremonially, other than drawing a salt circle around the cot and fire, and offering up the opening chant for the quest.

"Fire and Earth, sage and true, let me know how to follow you."

I repeated it three times, then closed my eyes. There was no need to get carried away. If the dragons needed to talk to me, they could speak anytime. This quest was more about appeasing my father and mother, than learning something big and relevant.

I knew I was dreaming when I looked down and noticed I was no longer in my own body. Instead, I was in the body of an old woman.

The old woman chuckled as the king pushed his way into her cave. "Woman, tell us your visions."

She ignored him, but I could tell it was mostly in good humor. I could hear her thoughts, or maybe it was more that I could feel them.

When both were seated, she spoke, "We must all take heed. Our children must remember what I'm about to say, for there shall be no more warnings. As I have already predicted, for a thousand years and then three hundred more after that, there will be no more seers."

The old woman had imparted her vision to the king's royal household multiple times, driving home how the gifts must be protected, and shared only among the women and a few select men who shared both the female and male spirit. That was the only way the craft could be preserved.

"When the dragons begin to wake, the new seer shall travel to a new world, and shall set up a village there between time and space. They will exist between the worlds of life and death, and shall console the dragons. One day, a dragon shepherd will arrive and lead the world back to the faith. This will be when it can be followed with no fear."

THREE

—·—

KYLE

S TILL TIRED FROM MY unexpected teleporting, I sat on the floor of my grandma's attic, alone with my thoughts and a chest full of keepsakes my grandma had set aside for me. I found it incredibly hard to believe Lance and Drew were like... *together*. Maybe I'd become so jaded about relationships, I just couldn't see when people fit or didn't.

I looked through the turtleback chest, and laughed as I came across an old board game Grandma and I used to play. And by play, I mean yelled at each other about the other cheating, then laughed until we were crying.

Oh... wow. She really was gone. It felt so surreal. She and I had been close. I'd tried to stop by her home from time to time, or travel with her to whatever destination she was going for whatever witchy thing she wanted to do.

That all more or less stopped when I started working on my dissertation. Fuck, why hadn't I spent more time here with her? I knew the answer deep down, though. Even though she was his opposite, being here still made me think of Dad and all that I'd lost when he'd cursed us. All that *we'd* lost. And it was mostly my fault. Had I not asked Lance and Crea...

I shook my head and quickly piled all the stuff back into the trunk before closing the lid. I had absolutely no place to store it, so I'd need to ask if Drew minded if I left it here for a while. I leaned back against the trunk and opened the small package Drew had plucked off his mantel and handed to me.

I smiled at the little ruby pendant. I'd always enjoyed divination, although it was mostly just fun for me. I never really took any of it too seriously. And now, as a scientist, I felt even further removed from it.

Regardless, I let the pendant swing. I already knew it had come out of her wedding ring. Lance and Crea had told me Grandma had used the stones from her ring to fashion them new ones to remember her by. Of course, they also said their rings held magical powers, but we hadn't gotten into the nitty gritty about that yet.

I was happy that I had so many fond memories of her. She'd been a live wire all my life. Truth was, I could see her in me all the damn time. Hell, in a lot of ways, I looked more like her than even Dad did. I was thankful that when I glanced in a mirror, I didn't see his face reflected in my own.

Although I hadn't seen him in person for many years, I could easily pick Dad out of a lineup. Grandma had framed family photographs all over her house... pictures that, I noticed, were no longer on display. Not that I could blame Drew for boxing them up. Even though they were close, why would he want another person's family photos up in his home?

I sighed. "Grandma, I will always love and miss you...
I just wish I'd..."

Dust lifted up off the floor with a breeze that defied
logic, and I chuckled, "Okay, okay... you aren't gone."

The air stilled and I smiled. "I still miss you though."

❖

I stared at my brothers in disbelief. "So, you think because you've shacked up with these two," I said, motion-
ing to Drew and Eli, "...that you are no longer cursed?
And what? Now I'm in the line of fire?"

Lance speared me with a look he usually saved
for courtroom cross-examinations. "*Shacking up with?*
Kyle, you've known the struggles we've had with relationships..."

"And you think magic has fixed it, and you and Drew
are going to live happily ever after?"

Drew chuckled, diffusing the rising tension. "No," he
answered for Lance, and put his hand over my brother's,
I think to shut him up. "Listen, we faced a foe that
wanted to kill us and almost did."

"As did we," Crea interrupted, glancing at his
boyfriend, Eli.

"But—" Drew continued, " we overcame it, and
we're all concerned you're about to face the same chal-
lenge."

"And all this is Dad's doing?" I said sullenly, sounding
childish even to myself. To be honest, I couldn't say why
this conversation was making me so angry.

Crea nodded, then said, "Look, Grandma gave us all a stone. Mine was emerald, and Lance's was a diamond. Each stone represents our elemental power."

I looked at him, but didn't respond.

He turned to Eli, and smiled in a way that caused even my jaded heart to skip a beat. "Eli, I love you with all that I have in me. You are my light... my savior..."

Before Crea finished speaking, a heart-shaped emerald tattoo lit up on his hand. And when I looked at Eli, the same had appeared on his opposite hand.

I glanced over at Lance and Drew, who were making heart eyes at each other as matching diamond-shaped tattoos glowed on their foreheads. They both leaned forward while whispering sweet words to each other, letting their tattoos touch.

"Ugh, okay, this is sappy as hell. I get it, you're in love, Grandma tattooed you with love... got it!"

I stood up and paced toward the living room's front window as my brothers and their mushy lovers... boyfriends... fiancés... *whatevers* chuckled behind me.

"It's great you've both found love, you've always wanted that," I said, turning back around to face my brothers. "But not me. I like being single. So, I doubt Dad's evil cantation or demon spirt is going to bother me."

I saw Drew frown as he looked toward the corner of the room. He nodded, then sighed. "Gwen says to tell you she's sorry you took after her."

"What's that supposed to mean?" I asked, feeling like I was being made fun of, even though I could feel Grandma's presence.

"She said you get your stubbornness from her."

I squinted toward where he'd seen her, and sighed. "Okay, whatever… but for real, I doubt it's going to be an issue. I'm perfectly content with my love life. Not everyone needs to be coupled up to be happy. Besides, if Dad's cantation is after me, I'll deal with it. It's not like I don't know how to use fire, and it's not like I don't know how to toss his sorry ass into a freaking volcano if I need to."

Both of my brothers were shaking their heads. Eli was just smiling.

"I doubt it'll be that simple, but you have us here, okay?" Crea said as Jennie, our niece, walked into the living room. She had been staying with her new girlfriend and Drew's neighbor, Scarlett, who was adorable and tough as nails. While I might not be good at picking love matches for my brothers, I knew Scarlett was perfect for Jennie.

The conversation slipped away from Dad's stupid curse and onto more fun things, like harassing my brothers and niece. A definite favorite pastime of mine.

I sat in Dr. Yvonne Agnes's office, angry enough to blow my top, not unlike Popocatépetl. "He had no right to cut me off, Yvonne. I'm mentioned in the grant!" I said, barely keeping myself from shouting. The quarter had just begun, and it looked like I'd be spending it stuck on campus.

Yvonne, one of very few professors I called by their first name, and who I considered my best friend, smiled in her usual, understanding way and shook her head. "You know as well as I do, he's the lead researcher. He's the boss, and you disobeyed his direct order."

"It had to be done!" I did shout this time, causing her to put her hands up.

"Regardless, you are off and out of the system. Dr. Fagan's exact words were to get your dissertation done, and he might give you access again."

"Might?" I asked, frustration flowing through me like molten lava.

"Might," she confirmed. "Listen, I shouldn't tell you this, and if you tell Dr. Fagan I told you, we'll both be up shit creek, but there's a job coming up through the US Department of the Interior. They want a volcanologist, but it has to be someone with a Ph.D. You have a foot in the door because of the grants you've worked on here... so, finish that dissertation already."

I slumped back into the seat. "I don't know if I want a job outside the university. I mean, this is my home," I said, hearing the whine in my voice.

"I know, but think of it this way. If you had a job working at the national parks in the Pacific Northwest and California, you'd have direct access to the school, and you may even be able to work from the school. But it's not even something to think about until and unless you complete your dissertation."

I sighed deeply before I thought about a possible way back in. "I need access to Popocatépetl's data if I'm..."

"Don't even try it. Both Dr. Fagan and I have read your paper. It's almost done. You have maybe a few more references to cite, but you already have all the data you need documented in your notes. So, Kyle, be done!"

"What about my things?" I asked.

Yvonne looked at me, brows furrowed. "Are you going to tell me why you left without them?" she asked.

I let out another long-suffering sigh, before saying, "Let's just say I had a family emergency and didn't have time to grab everything."

"Chemeketa?" she asked, and I nodded.

Yvonne was one of the few people in my life who knew about my family's abilities and our magical hometown. Well, her hometown, too, which was why I could tell her.

She got up from her desk and closed the office door. "Are you saying that you teleported?" she asked, whispering the last word. I nodded, and she looked shocked. "I've never heard of anyone teleporting that far. Was it because of the volcano's active status?"

I shrugged, and speaking as quietly as she had, said, "All I know is I was there one minute, and naked in my grandmother's garden the next."

"Wow, that's something you should speak to the Guild about. Are you going back to Chemeketa soon?" she asked. I rarely left Eugene, where the University of Oregon was located, unless it was to go work in the field.

I shook my head and deliberately left it at that. My own experience with my grandmother's ghost, as well as what my brothers had told me about the curse, had given me nightmares since I'd gotten home. Not that I was willing to admit that to anyone.

I kept seeing my dad's dark spirit, or cantation, standing over a volcano, causing it to erupt, then volcanic ash rained down as lava flows swept through Chemeketa, killing everyone in its path.

I knew most of the volcanoes along the coast were long extinct, but that didn't make the dream any less alarming.

"So, what? I'm stuck here until I've submitted my dissertation?" I asked, more to distract myself from remembering my horrible dreams than to get an answer... especially since I already knew that answer.

Yvonne nodded, and I sighed again in frustration. "Okay, damn. You know I have reasons not to get it done. For example, when I'm no longer a student, I won't be able to be Dr. Fagan's assistant any longer, right?"

She smiled. "And he and I agree, it's time for the baby bird to leave the nest. Finish your dissertation, send it to me so I can review it one last time, then be done with it. If you get it to me before the next quarter starts, you'll have more time to focus on fun stuff like the conference coming up in Vancouver. You know Dr. Fagan has been asked to give a talk. He's going to be too busy with Popocatépetl to have time to attend the conference, so if you were available..."

I chuckled. Both Yvonne and Dr. Fagan had my number. I loved teaching and giving lectures almost as much as I loved being in the field. I knew I needed to finish the work, but then I'd be set adrift, not unlike I had been when Dad had kicked us out of the house. Just the thought of it unsettled me.

Even all these years later, I still felt guilty. I'd wanted to tell our parents I was bisexual, and my brothers had wanted to support me, but our coming out had been met with intolerance and hatred. It'd been the single most horrible event in my life, even though it led to us living with our grandmother, and me learning about my abilities with fire.

As I left Yvonne's office and headed back to my own, I reached into my pocket and began to thumb the small ruby pendant Grandma had made me. Doing so gave me comfort, like she was still close by when I needed her.

Not that I believed the ring held magical powers that'd lead me to the love of my life, like Crea and Lance claimed theirs had. I was a sworn bachelor, and I had zero interest in getting married to a man or a woman. Nope, one night together was preferable, and two was as much as I ever wanted.

Sure, the curse had made Lance and Crea miserable. Anyone could see that, except maybe them at the time, but if anything, it made my life a hell of a lot better. My hookups always knew the terms going in, and I got to avoid all that mushy attachment stuff.

My thoughts were interrupted as I walked into my office and turned my computer on, and immediately got a message that a volcano in Tonga, the small Pacific island nation, had erupted again.

Pain seared through my head, and I heard a sinister laugh, followed by a voice saying, "It's only just begun."

FOUR

CONLEY

NIGHTMARE AFTER NIGHTMARE FOLLOWED the vision of the old woman. I watched in horror as generation after generation murdered people in horrific ways, all because they were accused of being witches.

I'd learned about such things in school, but experiencing them firsthand—at least, that's how it felt—was horrifying. First, I retched after watching a Catholic priest being disemboweled before his body was tied to four horses that were simultaneously whipped, ripping the man into pieces.

Then, the scene changed, and I saw Luna Raven, my third great-grandmother, arrive on this continent after months at sea. She was isolated, since the crew on the ship didn't trust her. I think they feared her.

I could feel her every emotion—her fear, loneliness, and worry that if she didn't reach her destination soon, she'd be in danger. She'd traveled here using only her intuition. I'd heard that story before, but in my dreams I witnessed it for myself, watching as she'd arrived in a port with two giant volcanoes visible from the water.

Since we'd been linked to the volcanoes in this dimension as well as Earth's, our schooling required we learn the names of all the volcanoes in our territory, which ran along the Pacific coast of North and South America. So, as Luna's ship docked, I recognized both Mount St. Helens and Mount Hood in the distance.

I could also feel how Luna sensed the other volcanoes around her. It was almost as if they were calling to her. As soon as Luna disembarked, she purchased a horse and began her journey south along the coast of Oregon. For days she traveled alone, with barely any food, and in danger of being attacked by lawless settlers and wild animals.

When she arrived at Chemeketa, I could feel her relief and assurance that she had reached her intended destination. Then, with the help of the Chemeketa villagers, she opened a rift that led her into the dimension between the veil and Earth. There, she created the village of Dóiteán and secured the passage between the two worlds.

My mind went blank then, and I assume I slept dreamlessly. The images had been intense, painful even. The fear I'd felt for and with my ancestor had taken a lot out of me.

I wasn't sure how much time passed before the images began again, and the old woman I'd first seen in my dreams stood before me, with Luna Raven beside her.

"You are the final phase of the prophecy. You are the reason we built Dóiteán. As darkness and light are thrown out of balance, it will wreak havoc in all dimensions, not just ours."

The three dragons, the same ones who'd appeared in my dreams since I was a child, stood above the women.

"Darkness comes, Conley," said a voice I recognized as Dubh, the black dragon. "If it is not stopped, it will force us to erupt. You must keep this from happening, Conley. Only you and the son of the darkness can save us."

"How am I to do that?"

The dragons had never smiled in my presence, but they all seemed to now. The sight was... unnerving. Regardless, what they said next terrified me more than any dragon ever had.

"You must beat the darkness back. The darkness is contained by love and commitment."

As a man who preferred other men, my options for finding love had been limited here in Dóiteán. I mean, the community had no problem with me as a person, but the men here left much to be desired, at least to me.

They certainly fancied each other well enough, but I was too... mouthy, one of them had told me. I tended to turn them all off, even if I was interested, which, unfortunately, I never was. Gael, the white dragon, had told me it was because the fire burned too brightly in me. It was my destiny to be mated with someone who had a similar power within him.

I'd read stories of virgins being cast into volcanoes, which had caused me to have more than one nightmare. When I brought it up to my parents, they assured me human sacrifice was never necessary. Nevertheless, I was still a virgin, and the weight of multiple worlds now rested on my shoulders to find love. In some ways, being a human sacrifice to the volcano seemed a far easier task.

FIVE

KYLE

Besides being my best friend and a brilliant scientist and university professor, Yvonne was a healer. Her grandmother was from Chemeketa, and therefore, I didn't have to hide my gifts from her. However, when I told her about the pain in my head and what the voice had said, she looked concerned. "You think this has to do with your father's curse?" she asked.

I'd told her about the curse early on. Yvonne, being a fire elemental herself, had worked with me to enhance my fire energy skills, particularly in relation to volcanic research. Often when dealing with fire energy, even the slightest emotional discharge could cause a fire to get out of control. So, knowing I was working with an active curse helped us avoid any unfortunate mishaps.

"Yeah, and my brothers have both had recent run-ins with my father's cantation. It seems the curse has taken on some sort of physical form. Anyway, they've both overcome it and apparently, now it's my turn."

She focused her gaze on me. "How did they overcome it?" she asked.

I shrugged. "They met men they fell in love with and, well, they fought against the cantation together and won."

Any trace of alarm on her face morphed into a familiar smirk. "Does that mean our most ardent bachelor is about to find love?"

"Hell no!" I said adamantly. "I have no interest in all that mushy romantic stuff. I'll end up having to fight it, but I'm not sure how."

"Do you mean fight the cantation or fight the romantic stuff?" she asked, and I couldn't help but glare at her. "You know, eventually even you may decide you want more to life than a quick fuck." She reached over and took my hand. "Just because you were shown the ugly side of love doesn't mean there isn't lots of the good stuff too."

Yvonne was old enough to be my mom, and I guess she filled that void from time to time. I couldn't have asked for a more understanding and supportive friend, which, unfortunately, also meant she could often see through my bullshit.

"You know, not everyone can find the perfect man like Sammy, get married, and live happily ever after in domestic bliss."

As always, her face took on a happy, dreamy look when I mentioned the love of her life, who she'd been married to for twenty-six years and counting. "We're lucky, but so are a lot of people. Don't just dismiss the chance, especially if you're getting a little boost from the universe."

I laughed. "If I get anything from my dad's curse, it'll be a butt-kicking. No, I've seen my brothers suffer for love. I've seen people who aren't even cursed suffer for love. I think what you and Sammy have is amazing, but it's not possible for all of us." When she put her hand up to contradict me, I added, "Not possible for people like me."

She shook her head. "Kyle..."

"I know, I know," I interrupted her again and stood to go. "I'll be in my office working on that stupid dissertation. Feel free to distract me at any time. I don't care for what reason. I'm open to distraction!"

"And that's why I'm going to guard the gate like a lioness guarding her cub!"

"Ugh," I said grumpily. "At least have lunch with me."

"If you can prove to me you've made progress, I'll buy you lunch."

I shook my head. "Okay, *Mom*. Just knock on my door when you're ready."

I moped back to my office, crashed into my chair, turned the ancient desktop computer on, and waited for it to boot up.

Like I'd told Yvonne, I'd resisted finishing my dissertation for good reason. It meant my life would change, and to be honest, I didn't want it to. I loved our little group here in the volcanology department—even Dr. Fagan, who could be a real hardass—and as soon as I graduated, I'd lose them, my place at the university... everything.

It's not that I hated change. It was just that change had always been hard for me. It didn't take talking to a therapist to know my feelings about that could be traced back to the night Dad had kicked us out of our home and his life.

It'd been amazing living with my grandmother, learning the craft and how to control the gifts I had, but it had come at a high price. Change didn't come without loss. That was the takeaway for me.

I halted that unwanted trip down memory lane to focus on the task at hand. A free lunch was riding on it, after all. My dissertation was about the overall impact volcanoes, especially frequently active ones, had on nearby populations. Not a new topic, but one that became more relevant as population density in areas around volcanoes increased.

Popocatépetl was the perfect example. Located in a heavily populated area, it had all the catastrophic potential of a dangerous volcano—projectile rocks, pyroclastic flows, lahars, and weather changes associated with an eruption. Its 1996 eruption had caused real damage and cost lives.

If and when one of the Cascade Range volcanoes would erupt, say Mount Rainier, the devastation could be beyond belief. Mount St. Helens showed us how susceptible we were, even in a largely unpopulated area. But Popocatépetl gave us a real glimpse of a volcano's destructive power in a more heavily settled environment.

I reread the paragraph containing the Popocatépetl information, details that weren't necessary, but had given me an excuse not to call the dissertation done, and stared at it for about ten minutes thinking about what it meant to turn it in. I thought about reading it again, but I had the damned thing memorized. I was just stalling.

I took a deep breath, composed a quick email to my dissertation committee, and submitted it for the final time.

I shut down the computer and let my mind drift from science to the other ways to keep volcanic activity in check. Magic. My grandmother hated when we called it that, saying magic was something for nothing, whereas drawing on the power of the elements required knowledge, skill, and respect. Was using it a viable solution to a great deal of problems around the world?

Not that anyone in Chemeketa would tell you they could or would interfere with the natural order of things, but an impending supervolcano eruption might be the exception to that rule. Yvonne and I had endlessly debated the ethics of such an intervention, and we frequently flip-flopped our positions. Each time, we concluded that if enough fire energy could be gathered in one place, the blast could and probably should be minimized.

The problem with that theory, of course, was that there just weren't enough fire elementals on the planet any longer to create a force strong enough to push back a supervolcano eruption, and as the years went on, our numbers continued to decrease.

Only a handful of people remained in the Fire Guild at Chemeketa, and only one was younger than me. Yvonne's father had been on the Guild until he passed before I was born, and her three cousins more or less kept it going nowadays. I sometimes I felt guilty for not being involved in the Guild, but doing so at a distance would've been difficult anyway.

A knock on my door caught my attention. That could only be Yvonne, coming to find out why, less than half an hour after I left her office, I'd turned in my much-delayed dissertation.

"What the hell?" she asked as the door opened.

I shrugged. "You convinced me, so I finished it."

She shook her head, and asked, "You're sure it's done? You don't want us to send any final feedback to you? I mean, you aren't self-sabotaging, are you?"

"Please, my pride wouldn't let me do such a thing, and you know it." I leaned back as I let my breath out. "I guess you and Dr. Fagan were right, it's time. I don't want it to be, but... well, I finally ran out of excuses."

She smiled at me from across my desk. "Moving on from here, it'll be great, I promise. I can see your future, or glimpses of it, and it looks spectacular."

I sat up then, curious what she meant. "What have you seen?" I asked.

She laughed. "Not any magical insights, but your innate talent, combined with your other more peculiar gifts, it all shines, Kyle. Now give me a hug. I'll play hooky and we'll grab lunch, then go get chocolate and coffee. You can tell me all about your reservations, and I'll pretend like they were valid enough for you to hold yourself back. It'll be fun."

I shook my head and thought about my friend. She didn't mince her words. That just wasn't her way, but she was intensely loyal, and despite what she'd just said, she was incredibly empathetic. Thank the gods I'd gone to school at U of O, and she'd been the first professor I had in my field. I couldn't imagine life without Yvonne in it.

SIX

— · —

CONLEY

"**T**RAVEL THROUGH THE PORTAL *to the other dimension?" I asked, the shock of the request reverberating through me. "I can't possibly…"*

"This is your quest, the purpose of this dream state," Luna *said. "You must find the son of the darkness. You must defeat the darkness in the Earth realm, and then you must bring him here to do the same."*

"And why would he follow me?"

"Because, Conley—" Dearg, the red dragon, said, "—he will find you sexy."

I could feel myself blush at the sexual energy emanating from Dearg. She had always represented sexuality to me. Some people in Dóiteán called her the temptress, so I figured it wasn't just me she had that impact on.

"Okay, I'll go, but what do I do if he refuses to cooperate?"

Visions of Dóiteán bathed in ash and death swirled through my head, followed by scenes of destruction in the Earth realm.

"You must not fail," Dubh said.

I nodded sadly, not at all happy about having to take on a quest that involved leaving my home. Not that I was welcome at home these days, but it was what I knew. I didn't want to be forced into a world that didn't accept us either, but if it meant saving our world...

I woke up alone in the cave, sweaty and starving. I had been out of it longer than anticipated, since all of my packed food had spoiled. Luckily, I found the emergency rations stored in the cave, which helped sate the worst of the hunger. Then, I bathed in the nearby hot springs, put my clothes back on, and began my descent from the great mountain.

I could feel the presence of all three dragons as I descended. Where I felt nothing less than trepidation, they were excited and pushing me with a sense of urgency. "Okay, okay," I muttered rebelliously, when one of them shoved me, and I all but stumbled. "I'm going, but, if you don't mind, I'd rather make it down the mountain alive."

I could hear the three chuckling in my mind. The villagers stopped when they saw me approaching. No one smiled, no one waved, but all of them stared as if I'd somehow grown a second head.

I looked down to see if maybe something had happened to make me look different, but to the best of my knowledge, nothing had.

When I reached my parents' house, my mother met me at the door crying. "Conley, we thought you were dead!" she said.

"Dead? Why?" I asked, and my father came and put his hand on my shoulder.

"It's so good to have you back home, son. But why did it take so long? Where did you go?"

"I was in the cave, just as we were taught," I said, confused.

Both my parents shook their heads, looking relieved, but equally confused. "No, son, we went there after you'd been gone for two weeks. We searched for you, but you were nowhere to be found. No trace of you remained. It was as if you were never there."

"You've got to be kidding. I *was* there, and I brought back news. I have to go on another quest. I can tell you everything that happened, but basically, I was told to go to the Earth realm."

"Conley, you've been gone for over a year!" my mother exclaimed as she hugged me tight before releasing me. "And now you're going to Earth? Through the portal? Why?"

"A year?" I fought to make sense of it. "No, I... Mama, it was a week at most. I was in the cave, and my food was still there, even though it wasn't in good shape when I woke up. It couldn't possibly have been a year."

Neither of my parents responded, and I could tell by the way they stared at me that I had, in fact, been gone that long. I felt my face and only had a small amount of scruff, no more than a few days' worth. "I don't understand."

"Did you have visions?" I heard someone ask from behind me.

I turned to see our village's spiritual leader, Guha Cho, standing in the open doorway.

I nodded. "Yes, a lot of them, but..."

He shook his head. "Son, time doesn't run the same for the dragons as it does here. We've had people lose weeks up there before, but never a year. Of course, my guess is the visions you had were intense and likely important to Dóiteán. Why don't you tell us what you saw? We'll know more about how to proceed after that."

I nodded and went the rest of the way into the house. Putting my pack on the floor, I sat across from Mr. Cho and my parents in the sitting room, and told them everything I could remember from the moment I lay down on the cot in the cave until I woke up. Then, I mentioned the dragons prodding me as I came down from the mountain.

"You say when you complained about going on another quest, they showed you an image of Dóiteán's destruction?" Mr. Cho asked.

"Yes, there's an imbalance between the darkness and the light. Apparently, the darkness is attempting to overpower the dragons both in this dimension and on Earth. Therefore, we must overcome it in both realms."

"And this son of darkness?" my mother asked. "He doesn't sound like someone you'd want to be around."

Mr. Cho put his hand up, and said, "You know, Aine, darkness and light are not enemies. They are meant to coexist. Just because this man is called the son of darkness doesn't mean he's evil or means harm to our world. If the dragons and your ancestor trust him, then we must do the same."

My parents sat quietly as Mr. Cho turned to me. "You must go, son, and the sooner the better. You have been called. Fulfill your destiny and bring the son of darkness back with you. We will prepare for your return."

I nodded and suddenly, feeling quite tired, stood to go. "I'm going to go to bed, then tomorrow I'll pack. If Langley is available, I'd like to speak to him since he's traveled through the portal to Earth several times. Maybe he can give me some insight into what I'm walking into."

Mr. Cho nodded. "That's an excellent idea. Why don't you all come to my home tomorrow, and we'll have breakfast together? I'll ask Langley to join us, as well as a few others who have crossed through the portal. Maybe they can help prepare you. I also know you'll need paper currency, and we keep some here for when our people cross over to buy goods."

I nodded, and the exhaustion from my journey down the mountain, as well as the realization a year had passed, wore on me. My room was just as I had left it; my parents hadn't touched it in my lost year, and it had a certain shrine-like feel to it now. I barely had time to think about how my poor mother and even my dad must've reacted when they thought something had happened to me.

Despite my concerns for them, sleep overtook me as soon as my head hit the pillow, and unlike my time in the cave, I had no dreams or visions, just a long, deep, and restful sleep.

I carried the heavy bag on my back as I walked along the river that flowed toward the sea. Langley, despite his age, led me most of the way, then as we approached the cave, he pointed toward its entrance and wished me luck. Mama had been beside herself that morning, not wanting to let me go. Dad hadn't been much better, except he tried to remain stoic.

"I'll be fine," I tried to reassure them. "Besides, now that you know I'm not dead, you can actually enjoy having the house to yourself."

My dad cringed, and I immediately felt bad. Before my vision quest, he'd been telling me I needed to move out so they could enjoy being empty nesters. I still couldn't grasp the time gap, and I could tell my time away had been exhausting and stressful for them. My mother had lost weight, and my dad's face had drawn tighter. Clearly, it'd been a lot for them to process.

I felt guilty about leaving again, but only a bit. Something had happened to me, too, while I'd been in that cave. A feeling of purpose had infused me that hadn't been there before. Now, it permeated my entire being. Just what that meant, I didn't know, but it felt good to have a purpose, especially after spending so many years of my life adrift and in a sea of ambiguity.

"You need to be careful when you come out of the cave. The Kels will meet you first. You must tell them from where you come. They'll understand and will escort you out of the forests and to the village of Chemeketa," Langley informed me.

I knew quite a lot about that village, having learned about it all my life through family stories and in school. Not long after Luna had created the portal that enabled her and others to cross through, the Chemeketa villagers had deliberately cast a spell to erase all memory of it for their own protection, knowing anything that bridged our worlds could be dangerous for all involved.

That didn't mean villagers didn't know about the other dimension or our existence, though, only that they couldn't access the portal themselves. Reportedly, the

Kels had never been participants in the village's political structure, so the spell hadn't worked on them. "That means they will be your guides," Langley had explained after escorting me to the cave, "...and if you need it, they can protect you. Just don't be too forthcoming when you get to Chemeketa. Unless you push the issue, they won't ask you where you come from. If they do, be honest, but let them ask you for information."

I left Langley behind without another word and walked into the cave. Aside from the gentle breeze Langley had warned me about, the transition was subtle. I honestly thought crossing between two worlds would be more intense.

I walked a long way through the cave. I wasn't necessarily claustrophobic, but I was definitely happy to reach the other side; it felt good to see daylight again. I was almost ready to burst into song about coming out of the darkness when I was physically struck.

The force of it flung me back into the cave, and I must have momentarily blacked out from the blow, because when I regained my senses, I could feel more than see that I was surrounded by a different form of darkness. This wasn't the benign absence-of-light darkness from the passage between worlds, this darkness was alive and had a malevolence to it. It fully intended to hurt me... kill me even.

I tried to yell, but before I could make a sound, the darkness tightened around my throat and began to choke me. Just as I was about to pass out again, I felt a sting that penetrated my chest right to my heart. I knew then I was going to die.

Before I completely blacked out, I saw smoke figures dancing in the air above me. They began to assault the darkness, pushing it back and causing it to release its grip around my neck.

I tried to struggle away as the whisps of smoke encircled me, but it was more than my mind or body could handle. *So much for saving the world*, I thought as I took what had to be my last breath.

SEVEN

KYLE

Yvonne and I had just sat down in the coffee shop with our coffee and chocolate truffles when her phone pinged. Her happy face melted into a frown after looking at the message. "Sorry, Kyle, I've got to go."

"Go where? What?" I asked, alarmed that maybe something had happened to Sammy or their daughter or, gods help us, their newborn granddaughter.

"It's Chemeketa. They've sent out an alarm."

When I continued to look at her blankly, she sighed. "It's part of the Fire Guild's protocols. Because there are so few of us, when the village is at risk or there's an emergency that requires the Fire Guild, those of us who live outside the village, but can get there quickly, are on-call."

"And they just called you up?" I asked. "Wait, my brother is the new mayor, or will be soon. If they're in danger, I'm coming too. Do you need to pick up Sammy?"

She shook her head. "No, he's not directly involved, but yeah, we could use your help. You're fire energy too. I'm surprised my cousins haven't already recruited you."

As we rushed out the door with cups and chocolates in hand, I explained that I'd avoided all that even when I'd lived with my grandmother.

Yvonne connected her Bluetooth when we jumped into her car and as soon as we got onto the road toward the village, she called someone who filled her in. "So, it's some hiker that's been attacked by a dark entity in the woods? Why do you need us?" she asked.

I couldn't hear the person on the other end, but Yvonne's eyebrows lifted. "Okay, I'm on my way, and I'm bringing Kyle Franklyn with me. He can help. We'll see you in about an hour and a half," she said, and hung up.

"What's going on?" I asked.

She hesitated for a moment. "Kyle, you're not a member of the Guild, so there are things I can't tell you, but I can say this. A man hiking in the great forests that surround Chemeketa was attacked by some type of evil entity, a darkness. It ended up poisoning the poor guy. The poison is magic-based, and it's killing his heart. The Guild is slowing it down until we arrive, but unless they can get a quorum, he won't make it."

Remembering my experience with my dad's cantation on Popocatépetl, an uneasy feeling coursed through me. Yvonne's description also sounded an awful lot like what like my brothers had described about their encounters with the darkness.

"How many is a quorum?" I asked.

"Thirteen is the optimum number, but I doubt they'll find that many. Seven is the minimum we need for this kind of magic, but nine is better."

"Are there enough Guild members who can come?"

She shrugged. "It's like most things, the older folks are all that remain in the area, and the younger generations have moved away or rejected their gifts altogether. We'll just have to wait and see."

With that, Yvonne changed the subject. I could tell it was to preserve the secrets of the Guild, but now my curiosity was getting the better of me. It took everything I had not to push for more information, but I respected her and her privacy enough not to pry.

When we finally arrived in town, we stopped at a home embedded in volcanic rock and standing high on an ancient lava flow that overlooked the ocean. We were rushed into a room filled with people. I sighed with relief when I counted nine. With Yvonne and me, that made eleven, which surely had to be a good thing.

"Join hands," an elderly man said. I recognized him, from years ago. He ran a jewelry store out of a small bungalow in downtown Chemeketa. I couldn't remember his name, but at the moment, it didn't seem very important.

I joined hands with Yvonne and an elderly woman I didn't know, and immediately felt the ring of fire we'd created surge through me. As the circle chanted words I didn't know, so I couldn't join in, I noticed the victim for the first time. We surrounded him as he lay on the bed.

His eyelashes were long, impossibly so, and his thick hair fanned out over the pillow. He also had rich dark skin and was truly the most handsome man I thought I'd ever laid eyes on, even with his eyes closed. Just as that thought came to mind, my heart began to hurt. At first it was a slight burn that quickly transformed into intense pain.

I cried out, but remembered my training, forced my-self to maintain the circle and kept holding the hands of the women at my sides. However, that didn't stop me from falling to my knees.

Yvonne looked down at me, concerned.

"My heart," I moaned, "Oh, my gods, it hurts so bad!"

The chanting around me rose as darkness enfolded me.

The pain was gone, but I was no longer in the room. Before me stood the injured man, looking perfectly healthy. Behind him were three dragon heads—one white, one black, and a red one that was smiling terrifyingly at me. "Um, are you going to eat me?" I asked, feeling slightly ridiculous.

"Not yet," the red dragon said, "...but if we decide to, I call dibs."

"Ignore her," the man said. "That's Dearg, she's always joking around."

"Playing with her food," the black dragon said.

"Guys, cut it out," the man said, sounding annoyed. "They don't eat humans. In fact, they aren't even real dragons, they're volcanoes."

"What?" I asked, confused. "Why are you dragons if you're... what?"

"They manifested as what my ancestors thought they looked like, but they're in this form so we can communicate with them better."

"Where are you from?" I asked, and the man hesitated.

"We're from a place called Dóiteán, but I ask that you don't ask me any more questions. I'm not supposed to talk to you about that, I don't think. Anyway, what happened to me? Why am I not dead?"

I shrugged. "They're healing you, but I'm not really a part of all this. I was just here to help, but I think I started feeling your pain, and the next thing I knew, I was here, with you and... them," I said, pointing at the dragons.

"Oh, son of darkness then?" he asked almost sadly.

"No, son of a jackass, but... well, I don't know, he was pretty dark. Um, are you going to be okay?" I asked and started to reach toward his chest, but snatched my hand back.

His soulful eyes tracked my movements before he nodded. "Yeah, I can feel myself waking up. You probably will too. I think most of the poison is gone, which is good, because that was the most pain I've ever felt."

"Yeah," I said, rubbing my chest over my heart. "I got a taste of it, but that was quite enough...."

Just as I heard the chanting again, I was transported back to the room. My chest still hurt, but the pain wasn't quite as unbearable. Yvonne and the woman on my other side were kneeling next to me. I looked over at Yvonne, and she winked but didn't stop chanting. I was still too weak to get up, but could see that on the bed, the man I'd seen in my vision was regaining consciousness. As his eyes opened, he immediately made eye contact with me.

I wasn't sure if it was all the night's events or something else, but the moment his eyes met mine, the pain in my heart subsided, and in its place was a thrill of excitement. It was almost as if I'd finally found what I'd been looking for, which was stupid and ridiculous, so I shoved the thought out of my head.

The poor guy was only awake for a few moments, just long enough to look at me, before his head fell back and his eyes closed. Asleep again. That was good, according to the jeweler, who'd introduced himself to me as William Shepherd after the group finished their ceremony and cleansed the circle.

"So, you connected with him then?" Mr. Shepherd asked.

I nodded, but was reticent to add much about what I'd seen, so I went with the most benign details. "I saw him in a vision or something? He said he's from Dóiteán?"

The group around us gasped, and suddenly I thought maybe I should've led with the dragons. "Dóiteán? So, it's true then?" someone asked.

"What's Dóiteán?" I asked. "He told me not to ask many questions about it."

"And that's right," Mr. Shepherd said. "We're sworn not to disclose that information, but if he chooses to tell you, it's his story to tell."

I decided not to share any more about my vision at that point. Maybe it was me being a bit petty, because they were withholding information from me, but it also felt like the dragons weren't something I should talk about, at least not without their permission.

"How are you feeling?" Yvonne asked.

"Fine, it's like I connected with him and could feel his pain, but I don't have the residual exhaustion. Poor man seems to be wiped out."

"He will, unfortunately, be wiped out for some time. He's stabilized, but not cured," said an older woman who approached us. "Hi, I'm Rose Shepherd. I was friends with your grandmother, and I'm the official leader of the Fire Guild in Chemeketa. You've met my husband, William, and this is our son, Philip." She gestured to the young man standing next to her, who gave me a small wave hello.

"I recognize you, Philip. We were in high school together, but you were a few years behind me."

He nodded and smiled. "Yes, and too shy to hang out with seniors, I'm afraid."

I chuckled. "I wasn't shy about anything in high school, so not many freshmen were willing to introduce themselves to me my senior year."

Philip's gaze drifted from me to the sleeping man. "Thanks for coming tonight. There was no way we could've handled this on our own."

"No, I suspect not. Do you know what happened to him?" I asked.

"We have our suspicions, but we'll meet with the mayor and the former mayor tomorrow, as well as the Kel leader. The Kels are the ones who found him. After processing that amount of poison, he'll need a lot of rest, but for now he should be fine. Hopefully we'll learn more after he wakes, and we can speak with him."

I nodded, but deep down I thought I already knew who was behind the attack. I'd need to talk to the new mayor, my brother Lance, as well. Things were coming into focus now, and I didn't like what I saw... some innocent man being pulled into my dad's wretched curse. *Fucking Dad!* Why couldn't he just leave us the hell alone?

EIGHT

CONLEY

AFTER THE ENCOUNTER WITH the handsome man, I drifted into a dreamlike state and found myself back home in Dóiteán, but instead of the cold rainy weather that plagued our village in winter, it felt like midsummer.

A meadow stretched between the dragon mountains and butted up against the river. The ground there was way-too rocky and the topsoil so shallow it was no good for agriculture. When Luna and her followers first arrived, they ignored the meadow and built in an area with more fertile ground.

For me, however, the meadow was pure heaven. I'd spent many days lying among the wildflowers in the middle of the field, staring up at the sky as insects buzzed around me and the river gently flowed nearby. This was where I first encountered the dragons. Gael first, as she was the gentlest. She'd sit next to me for hours just silently pondering the world like I did.

Eventually, as I grew older, she introduced me to Dubh, who was significantly larger, and a great deal scarier. Then, when I went through puberty, they both introduced me to Dearg. As an adult, I spent many an hour sitting in the meadow looking out over the three mountains off in the distance while their dragon forms kept me company.

I thought that was what annoyed my dad the most. I was a daydreamer, not a leader like he'd wanted me to be. Mama told me repeatedly how our culture valued hard workers, which was her way of telling me I annoyed her as well.

Finding myself back home didn't really surprise me. I knew I was dreaming, but I could tell there was a difference between the days I'd spent daydreaming my life away and the dream state I was in now. The dragons were the only thing that felt the same.

"Why does the darkness move there?" I asked Dubh, pointing out across the meadow.

The dragon sent feelings of concern and dread. "It lurks even in Dóiteán now. I suspect it came through the portal when it pierced your heart."

"So, this is my fault after all?"

"No," Gael said. "He was waiting for an opening, Had it not been you, it would've been Langley. It was just too dark for us to see."

"So, what do I do now?" I asked.

"It is the remnants of a curse, and all you can do is fulfill your mission."

"You mean, finding my soulmate and dragging him to Dóiteán, to what? Fight the curse?"

They sat silently, and I knew they weren't quite sure of the answer. I wasn't either. I thought of the handsome man who'd stood at the foot of my bed, then come to me and the dragons in a vision. Could he be the one? If so, I certainly didn't mind looking at him.

Sandy-blond hair hung long over his shoulders and into his eyes, but in a way that felt carefree and maybe even a bit boyish. He was taller than me and his body was thinner than mine, but I could tell the lean muscles lurking beneath his clothes were the result of working for a living. I couldn't say I hadn't wanted to touch him. I certainly had. Even in my innocence, I could tell when a man was... desirable.

I looked out over the meadow just in time to see an older woman walking toward us. Clearly, she could see the dragons, because as she approached, she nodded at each of them and bowed slightly before addressing me. "Hello, I'm Gwen."

I could tell the woman was a spirit not of this world. She appeared confident, and didn't carry the same woeful aura as the spirits I'd seen stuck in the dimension Dóiteán occupied.

Spirits could communicate easy enough in Dóiteán, although most didn't, so I wasn't alarmed by the woman's presence.

"What can we do for you, Gwen?" I asked.

She chuckled. "It's me who has come to aid you, Conley."

I nodded, but didn't speak.

She turned toward the darkness hovering at the edge of the meadow. "Unfortunately, that's my son's doing. In Chemeketa, it's an actual cantation, although here it appears to be only a cloud." She looked back at me, and said, "Before I can transition through the veil, I must help make it right. It's what I've committed my spirit to. I can also sense you're part of that."

"It attacked me," I said, trying to keep the accusation out of my voice.

She nodded sadly. "And given the chance, it will attack you again. You pose a great threat to it, Conley of Dóiteán. I'll help guide you and my grandson toward stopping it." Then, she lifted her gaze to look behind me where the dragons waited. "Hello, dragons of Dóiteán. It's a great honor to meet you."

The comment about her grandson didn't escape me, but my gut told me this wasn't the time to bring up particulars. Not, at least, until I was able to speak to the dragons about her. Spirits were known to be deceiving and that darkness was, according to the dragons, some sort of curse. I wanted to know what her involvement was before I opened myself up to her.

The emotions the dragons sent toward her was acceptance, which did tell me she was someone to be trusted. I believed the three of them more than any human. Stories were told of bad people who'd slipped through the portal from Earth and spirits slipping through the veil to Dóiteán, only to be banished by the dragons shortly after they arrived.

I wondered why they didn't just banish the darkness, but somehow, I figured they weren't able to. At some point, maybe that would become clear.

"Thank you, Gwen. I don't quite understand why we're here, but you're welcome to keep us company."

"Back there... you're still not out of the woods. When you were attacked, the darkness pierced your heart. So, our people, the Fire Guild, are keeping you alive while

you heal. When you wake, maybe we can begin the process of banishing the darkness."

I nodded. "Then, I suppose we wait."

Gwen smiled. "You will not wait alone, but unfortunately, my time is limited even in this plane of existence. He will come soon..."

She disappeared, just like that, and I turned toward the dragons and shrugged. When they didn't respond, I sighed inwardly and lay back on the ground, letting myself drift to sleep.

NINE

— · —

KYLE

THE OLDER MAN SITTING in front of me identified himself as Katan Manning, the former mayor. Of course, I remembered him from my days in Chemeketa, and how he'd tried to convince my grandmother to pressure me into joining the Fire Guild. Of course, Grandma railed against anyone telling her what to do, though it didn't stop her from trying to do so in her own way.

The Guild had extended an invitation to join when I graduated from high school, which I'd declined, because I knew Chemeketa would never be my home. It felt wrong to offer all the old people in the Guild false hope.

Katan paused and looked at my brother, Lance, and said, "There is another dimension that exists between our reality and the veil. There are very few ways to access that dimension from this one. One of those exists here in Chemeketa. When our people came to Chemeketa, it was clear there was great unrest among the volcanic forces. So much so that it was unsafe to live in these parts, as a volcano could erupt at any time. A young woman traveled here from Ireland in the late eighteen hundreds and was guided to our village when it was still a new settlement."

Lance nodded but didn't interrupt. "Long story short, with the help of the Fire Guild that had formed, she created a portal between our worlds. They call the place on the other side Dóiteán."

I wanted to chuckle, because Katan paused for maximum effect. Not that this wasn't interesting or dramatic, but you could tell he was enjoying telling the story.

"For more than a century, we have worked to keep the dragons, as they call them, at peace... well, as much as they can be at peace. We still have eruptions, of course, but their impact is minimized because of Dóiteán's involvement."

"So, what? You're saying that for generations, descendants of our town's founders have been in an alternate dimension preventing volcanic eruptions?" I asked.

Katan nodded. "I'm sure the young man will have more information and answers to your questions. I only know the basic facts and only because I was mayor. Lance, of course, is now privy to the information and the Kels as they keep vigil over the portal. Still, I wouldn't have told you, except I dreamed of Gwen last night, and she told me I should fill you in too. You... seem to be part of the reason this man has come."

Katan squared me with a look, before continuing, "But, son, you mustn't tell anyone about the portal. If the wrong people were to get access to something as powerful as that..."

"It would be disastrous," I finished for him.

"Yes." He nodded.

"I won't share the information, it's safe with me, but I'm not sure how I'm involved."

Lance sighed, and I looked over at him. "You know, Kyle. It's likely this is to do with Dad and his cantation, the same one Crea and I had to fight."

I shook my head, and scoffed, "And I'm just supposed to fall madly in love with this random man, and what? Marry him, have kids, and live happily ever after? You know that's not how I operate and it's not even something I want."

"I don't know, Kyle," Lance said. "Drew could probably help us see, or someone like our neighbor Alegia, who has scrying skills, but I'm not sure how to use them, since they aren't allowed to know about the other dimension."

"Well, I'll face what comes, but none of you should expect me to ride off into the sunset with this man or any of that nonsense. Dad cursed us, but I don't think of it as a curse. I'm just not the marrying kind."

I stood up and forced myself to remember my manners, thanking Katan, then patting Lance's shoulder. "I'm going home. I don't think you need me anymore, but if Dad's... *whatever* comes back to haunt me, I'll let you or Crea know, but for now, I'm going back to work, if they'll let me," I muttered.

I know I left them confused, but I wasn't playing matchmaking games, and sure as hell not with a man who'd come through some mystical portal, no matter how good-looking he was. Damn, they were all probably still stuck in the eighteen hundreds. I liked my men to know what the hell they were doing, and I certainly didn't get off on *thees* and *thous*.

Yvonne said she'd wait for me to finish the meeting, but I was done with Chemeketa. I'd forgotten what the weight of the expectation felt like–the desire for me to join the Fire Guild and follow in my grandmother's footsteps or whatever they wanted me to be. I'd chosen to become a researcher, a scientist, and I'd be damned if I didn't choose to carve my own path.

"Damn," I said out loud as the frustration hit me again as I walked out of the Grange House.

"Um, you okay?" Yvonne asked.

"Sorry, just frustrated. It's just the old *we need you here* crap I used to get from Grandma and her friends. I know I'm selfish, but damn. I don't want all that."

She reached over and squeezed my shoulder. "It really isn't your destiny either. I think you'd die in Chemeketa. It's an amazing place, truly, and even Sammy and I know we'll eventually retire here. But it's like any small village struggling to survive. They see someone younger than sixty and want to begin giving you jobs."

"Exactly. Jobs I don't want."

"Have you figured out what you do want?" she asked.

"Don't you start, especially right now. In fact, change of subject. I need ice cream, and then when I get home, I need alcohol."

⚜

Despite what I'd told Yvonne, I was getting tired so when I got home, I decided to forgo the alcohol, opting instead for a shower and bed. Now that my dissertation was turned in, I needed to figure out what came next in my life, but I knew Chemeketa wasn't it. Unfortunately, I also knew that neither was the university.

Life was changing and I hated that, but change, just like shit, happened, right?

It took me a while to fall asleep, but when I did, I dreamed.

I found myself in the middle of a beautiful meadow with a little river flowing on one side and a forest on the other. Three large conical volcanoes towered in the distance.

I turned around and came face to face with the three dragons from my previous vision. I somehow knew they didn't pose any danger, but still swallowed hard, remembering how the red one had called dibs on eating me.

Looking down, I saw the man—whose name I still didn't know—lying in the grass, out cold, but wearing a peaceful expression. "Should I wake him?" I asked, thinking maybe the dragons would answer.

The black dragon, the largest of the trio, let out a huff that sent puffs of smoke pouring from its nostrils. "You resist what must be. We don't understand why."

I felt my face flush. "I should have a choice about who I fall in love with, shouldn't I?" I asked, angry and a bit frustrated.

"You always have a choice, but why make that choice before you've even gotten to know him?" the white dragon asked.

"I don't like being pushed into something against my will."

"*Even if he's tasty?*" the red dragon asked, and I could feel her humor. "*You like him. I can tell by the way your body reacted the first time you saw him.*"

I shook my head. "It doesn't matter if I like him or not, I don't... well..." I struggled to know how to phrase it so three dragons might understand. "I don't want to be tied to him or anyone."

All three dragons laughed. "*You already are,*" they said in unison. Then, just like that, they vanished.

I looked down as the man at my feet began to stir. "Hi," he said as he sat up. "I must've fallen asleep."

I smiled at him, even though I felt more like yelling and throwing things than smiling. But I tried to keep my toddler temper tantrums to a minimum these days.

"Are you okay?" I asked, wondering if he was still in pain from his injuries.

"I'm okay, I guess, although... why are you in my dream?"

This time, my smile was genuine. "That I can't say. I went to bed and found myself here, with you."

"You must be my guide. I was told my ancestor had one when she came to Dóiteán. I'm Conley, by the way. It's nice to meet you."

"Yeah, nice to meet you now we aren't in excruciating pain. I'm Kyle."

Conley smiled, and I'd be damned if my breath didn't hitch at the sight. Luckily, he didn't seem to notice. "Would you like to sit?" he asked. "Or go for a walk?"

I nodded, and although it was clear this was a dream, I could sense the significance of our spending time together.

"So, why are you here?" I asked, sitting on the warm aromatic earth.

"I'm not exactly sure, just that when I went on my vision quest, I was told to travel to the Earthly realm to help fight off a great darkness that threatened to disrupt the balance between our worlds."

"And how is crossing dimensions supposed to do that?" I asked.

He shrugged. "Not sure. I'm not even sure the dragons know, but that's what I was told to do." He hesitated for a moment, then said, "I'm supposed to meet my soulmate in this quest... is that you?"

He blushed adorably, and if I wasn't so freaking threatened by that question, I might've enjoyed getting to know him better, but as it was, I had no interest in diving into that pit.

"Um, no... probably not. If I were to guess, you're looking for someone much more connected to Chemeketa than I am, and most likely a fire energy at that."

"Do you know of such a man?" he asked, looking hopeful.

I already had a feeling, but his response confirmed my suspicion that Conley was gay. Staring into his beautiful eyes, I'd be damned if I didn't almost admit that I could be his man, but I couldn't in good conscience give him false hope that I was the commitment kind.

So, I had to think fast... who among the Chemeketa fire elementals could pass for a possible love interest? Only one man—the Fire Guild's lone non-senior citizen male member—came to mind.

"Philip?" I said, which sounded more like a question than an answer. "Um, yeah, there's Philip. He's a few *years younger than me and a fire energy, and was part of the healing circle after you were attacked."*

"Philip," he repeated, and I felt an unwarranted spike of jealousy at hearing the name roll off his lips. "I'm not even sure how old I am exactly. I sort of lost a year while on my vision quest. I went into the cave and didn't come back out for a year, although to me, it only felt like a week."

"Ouch, you got cheated out of a year of your life?"

"Almost. I do remember that one week," he said. I could tell he was teasing, and it made me feel strangely at ease.

"I guess that counts. Anyway, what do you do in Dóiteán? I was told where you're from, but not much else."

"Oh, okay, I was told most people didn't know about it." That seemed to puzzle him, but he shook it off, and continued, "Officially, I'm my father's apprentice. I'm expected to take over the leadership of our village, but in reality, I'm just the village errand boy. I run where they tell me and do whatever is needed."

"And you talk to dragons?" I asked.

"Yeah, and I know that's supposed to be the entire reason we're in Dóiteán, but I've known them most of my life. To me, they're more like invisible friends than creatures I'm supposed to be working with... or for."

I smiled. "The red one is quite the character."

He rolled his eyes, which I had to admit was kind of cute. "You have no idea. She used to embarrass the crap out of me when I was young. She still can if she tries."

"Yeah, I kinda like her."

"I'm sure she likes you too. You're her type."

I laughed. "And what is that?"

Conley blushed. "Let's just say she likes tall men with lots of muscles."

"Oh, nice compliment." For a moment, I wanted to say more, then remembered this was all a setup. We were practically on an arranged date, and as much as I'd like to think he was genuinely flirting, he was probably just being polite. So, instead, I changed the subject. "Why don't we take that walk?"

I liked Conley, and I liked the sense of peace I felt in this dream state. We were in a meadow by a river, and the sunlight warmed my skin. The smells were amazing, almost amplified, as was the sound of the wind blowing through the wildflowers and the water flowing over the rocky riverbed.

It was romantic as hell, and that was exactly why I was determined to keep Conley at arm's length.

I woke up after Conley and I had strolled along the river, then said our goodbyes. It was all so perfectly controlled that I just felt managed. Ugh, I was so not playing this game, even if three dragons were behind the matchmaking. They were scary and intimidating, but so was my grandmother when she had matchmaking on her mind, and I'd managed to avoid her meddling.

Even though Conley was handsome, smart, and sexy as hell, I didn't need or want a lifetime lover. No, thank you very much!

Ten

Conley

"*I* *LIKE HIM*," *I told Dearg, "But he said he isn't the one. Not my soulmate." She didn't respond, but I could feel her disappointment.*

Oh well, I couldn't control fate. I did think Kyle was better looking than any man I'd ever met, but he probably didn't fancy me that way, which was okay. I just enjoyed being around him, and in time might even consider him a friend.

Over the next few days, he began showing up when I woke in the mornings. I knew my body was still asleep, stuck in a sort of limbo between reality and dreaming, and maybe that was why I was here in Dóiteán. I had to admit, even if it meant lingering in the dimension between life and death, I was glad the rest of my village wasn't here.

Regardless, I started looking forward to Kyle's visits. We talked about our lives. Mine was boring, so mostly I just deflected the conversation back to him. He was fascinating. He told me he was a scholar studying in a large university.

We had one university like that, where our scholars studied. Mostly, it was just a bunch of old men arguing with each other about how best to please the dragons, or how to use certain fire abilities.

What Kyle described sounded much more enriching. I sat fascinated as he told me about a large volcano, larger even than Dubh, that was erupting in Mexico.

He also talked about how important ongoing research was to keep people safe when a volcano erupted. Of course, I couldn't disagree since that was what my entire civilization was based on. We, of course, approached things differently.

He enjoyed the stories I told about how we celebrated each holiday by pulling energy out of the dragons and redistributing it into our infrastructure, giving us similar luxuries to those in his dimension—like electric lights and running water, purified and clean enough to drink.

"The dragons provide for our needs, while we keep them in balance, it's a win-win."

"I wish more people did that with volcanoes in my world," he said, then smiled at me, and my heart gave a little leap.

I probably shouldn't be having heart palpitations over one man when I was supposed to be falling for another. So, when Kyle disappeared, I decided I would start asking him questions about Philip the next day. Maybe if I could learn more about the man, my apparent soulmate, I would feel prepared for meeting him once I woke up.

Not that I had control over when I woke, but I felt pressure from the dragons to move things forward. They visited me less and less. At first, I thought it was because of my time with Kyle, but I could now feel the strain they felt from the darkness as it drifted closer and closer to them.

The old woman, the one named Gwen who I'd seen when I'd first fallen into this dream state, also showed up again. She was always surrounded by the darkness, which scared me, especially since I could tell it scared her too.

"You must talk to him about the darkness," she urged me. "You must tell him time is running out."

I nodded respectfully, as I was taught to do when speaking with elders, but it didn't really convey my thoughts. I wasn't comfortable around this woman, and although I could tell she was harmless, the darkness that clung to her certainly wasn't.

That was the other thing I'd have to ask Kyle tomorrow. If he was my guide, which he must be, given our connection despite not being soulmates, he'd be able to connect with the healers on his side. Even if my body wasn't totally ready, maybe they could use their powers to wake me up. I needed all the time I could get to complete my quest—to meet and fall in love with the son of darkness—before it was too late.

ELEVEN

KYLE

EVERY NIGHT, AS SOON as I drifted to sleep, I ended up in the meadow with Conley. Now that I was becoming a regular visitor, he was awake when I showed up.

We spent our time together hanging out, just enjoying each other's company. Him telling me about his life and aspirations, me telling him about mine. He let me geek out about volcanology, which was truly the way to my heart, and I enjoyed learning about the dragons and their relationships.

When I arrived tonight, though, Conley was clearly troubled.

"Have you noticed the darkness that grows ever more present in the East?" he asked, pointing toward the mountains.

I nodded. I'd seen it when I first arrived and had watched it grow with every visit. I'd known it was my father's cantation, as my brothers had called it. But, unlike my brothers, the darkness hadn't been as threatening to me as the stories they'd told about their fight against it.

I took that as a good sign, but I could feel its malevolence as it drifted toward the volcanoes. I could also feel the energy of the villagers who occupied this dimension fighting it, and how it continued spreading despite their efforts.

"Conley, do you know what that darkness is?" I asked.

"No, just that it wants to destroy us. The dragons told me there was an imbalance between darkness and light..." He hesitated for a moment. "My people embrace the darkness, knowing it's part of our existence. Without dark, there can be no light, and vice versa. But, when there's an imbalance, it puts everyone at risk. Have the healers in your dimension told you when I'll wake?" he asked.

I shook my head. "No, I haven't asked. I can call my brother when I wake up. Or maybe ask Yvonne, my friend who was with me the first night we met."

"Yes, please do, and I would like to know more about this Philip. I was told he'll play an important part in our overcoming the darkness."

I bristled at the sudden change of topic. I already felt guilty about deceiving Conley, who I had to admit I was growing fonder of with every visit. I never should've tossed Philip's name out as a possibility, but I didn't think Conley would glom onto it so hard either. I knew Philip wasn't even gay, let alone a "son of darkness" as Conley had described his soulmate, but I also didn't like the thought of Philip filling a void between us, which, of course, just made me stupid.

I nodded. "I'll ask about both tomorrow and let you know."

Conley sighed and sat on the ground. When I sat next to him, he said, "I'm afraid, Kyle."

"Of what?" I asked, letting my shoulder bump his.

He looked at me for a moment, as if he were weighing his options in telling me or not, and shook his head. "I... well, I'm a bit of a freak. Can I confide in you? As my guide?"

I smiled at the adorable man next to me, and this time I let my shoulder brush against his and stay there. "Of course, tell me whatever you like."

"I... well, this Philip, he's supposed to be my soulmate, but..." He took a deep breath. "The men in Dóiteán, they never appealed to me. Most wanted a mate who wasn't so... dramatic as me. But, I can't change who I am, nor do I want to."

Unwilling to compromise who he was—a man after my own heart. I couldn't help but chuckle. "You aren't nearly as dramatic as some I've dated."

He didn't smile, but rather leaned into me harder. "I'm a virgin, Kyle," he said in nearly a whisper.

I stared at him a moment before he began to blush. "I... well, are they not tolerant of gay people in Dóiteán?" I asked.

He shook his head, his blush deepening. "No, all manner of sexual orientation is accepted in our culture. Relationships and getting married, that's what's valued most. My mother is the worst at threatening to find me a husband," he said, then laughed nervously. "She's always saying in her mother's native India, parents find spouses for their children. They call them arranged marriages."

"That's terrifying," I said. I was fully aware of arranged marriages, but never for gay couples. Suddenly my grandma's futile attempts at playing the meddlesome matchmaker didn't seem so bad.

"You have no idea. My mother tried fixing me up with so many horrible men, eventually I flat-out refused to meet any more. Not that I'm doing a very good job of finding someone myself." He sighed again. "Kyle, I'm not sure this Philip will want me. I'm not the best looking, and I'm inexperienced."

"Wait, what? You think you aren't good-looking?" I asked, unable to hide the surprise in my voice.

"No. Just look at me," he said, gesturing to his beautiful face. "My features are all out of whack. I'm tall and awkward... I inherited the worst features of both of my parents."

I stopped him from talking by putting my hand on his cheek and stroking it with my thumb. "You are one of the most handsome men I've ever met, Conley. Your eyes are so light brown, they're almost green. Your complexion is so smooth I can hardly keep myself from touching you. Any man would be lucky to have you."

Conley stared at me in disbelief, but ever so slightly leaned into my touch. "I-I think you're just trying to make me feel better."

That was too much. I leaned over and coming within a hair's breadth of his lips, glanced into his eyes for permission. When they heated, I closed the distance and kissed him. I curled my hand around the back of his neck and let my mouth taste him like I'd wanted to from the moment we met, although I'd been resisting it with all I had in me.

He moaned as my mouth traveled up his jaw and my tongue explored the soft skin under his ear, and I wanted... no, I needed to take more. Take what I'd forced myself not to even acknowledge I wanted until now.

"Wait... no," he said, and pulled away. "I-I do want you, Kyle, clearly." He gestured down at the bulge in his trousers. "But, I'm destined for Philip. You said so yourself."

I let myself fall back against the ground. Damn, I should've known this would come back to bite me hard in the ass. "I lied," I admitted, looking up at him and seeing a bewildered expression cross his face.

"I-I'm not following."

"Philip, to the best of my knowledge, is straight. He also has a girlfriend, at least that's what his cousin, my friend, told me."

"So, who is my... wait, you? You are who the dragons and the old woman spirit, Gwen, told me about? The son of darkness?" I couldn't tell if it was shock or hurt I heard most in his voice, but I didn't like either one.

I sat back up and shrugged. "Maybe," I said, and held my breath before letting it out slowly. "Likely. And, I didn't know my grandmother had been to see you... although I'm not surprised."

Conley stood up. "You... you deceived me, Kyle. Why? To make fun of me? The awkward man who admitted he's too undesirable to have ever had a lover?"

He turned his back and began to walk away as I scrambled to my feet to stop him. "Wait, Conley. It wasn't like that, it's... "

"It's what?" He turned on me, practically yelling. "You're a liar, Kyle. I trusted you. Trusted you with some-

thing so important to my people, my entire world. I'm such a fucking failure!" He closed his eyes briefly, clearly in pain. "Please, go," he said, holding up his hand to stop me as I began to walk toward him.

"But..." I stammered.

"No. Please, go," he said again.

I stepped away from him and could feel myself returning to my own world. When I looked up toward the eastern sky, the dark clouds had grown, as if they were gaining power from our argument.

I didn't wake up like I usually did. Rather, still in my dream state, I was back at Popocatépetl. It wasn't the volcano I'd known in real life, though. Instead, it was an angry twist of exploding lava and ash clouds. I gazed out across the burned landscape and saw utter destruction—villages and cities on fire, vegetation destroyed, and lifeless bodies scattered, encased in ash just like in Pompeii.

I heard the laughter as I looked up and saw the darkness riding the back of a skeletal dragon. I somehow knew—I could feel it—that the dragon was Popocatépetl, and the darkness was driven by my father. "I win," it roared, then cackled with laughter. "I win!"

I woke up sweating. I immediately grabbed my phone and checked online to see if Popocatépetl had erupted again, and was relieved to see that it hadn't. Just then, fierce shaking rocked my home. "Earthquake!" I yelled out loud. *Damn, Mount Hood,* I thought.

I could see in my mind's eye the white dragon and, for the first time, understood the white dragon in Dóiteán was actually Mount St. Helens. The black dragon, being the largest, was probably Mount Rainier. And the red?

I wasn't quite sure, maybe Mount Hood, maybe one further south. I'd concentrate on that later. For now, I needed to figure out why we were having earthquakes.

Of course, I shouldn't feel the impact of Mount Hood, not here in Eugene, so that comforted me some. But the South Sister Volcano—part of the Three Sisters volcanic region in central Oregon? Quite possible. I opened up the geological website and checked to see if there was any activity around me, but nothing had been reported.

So, just my imagination then. That thought was quickly kicked aside when another, larger quake hit. "Fuck," I said, scrambling out of bed to dive under my desk just in case, and immediately dialed Yvonne.

"Did you feel that?" I asked just as the shaking stopped.

"Yep, trying to figure out the source."

"Could it be a volcano not on our radar, or is it just a quake?"

"Not sure. Meet me at my office, we can investigate there."

I didn't bother with a shower. Instead, I brushed my teeth, threw on some clothes, and dashed to the university as fast as I could.

The quakes hadn't been strong enough to cause damage, but they were real enough. My instinct told me not only were they very real, but also that they had everything to do with me.

"It was a two-point-one," Yvonne said as I rushed into her office. She lived a lot closer to the university than I did, so she was already there when I arrived.

"It felt stronger to me than that. Was it just a quake?" I asked, and she gave me a quizzical look.

"Why would you assume it was anything but?"

I closed her door and explained what had happened, what had been happening, in my dreams.

"Shit, Kyle, you should've... I don't know what, but maybe not lie to someone who might prevent us from having a volcanic disaster?"

"I don't want to be pushed around, Yvonne. I don't have to have a relationship just because..."

She put her hand up. "You always have the right to make your own choices, but there are many types of relationships, Kyle. Look at ours. We've been friends for six years, and there's nothing romantic about it, but we are close. You and Conley sound like you were getting close, too, and now you've betrayed his trust. Why? 'Cause you don't want to be forced to date a hunky man from a different dimension? Try being his friend first."

I chuckled despite myself. "He is a bit of a hunk, huh?"

"And your freaking type, too." She walked over and put her hand on my shoulder. "But, Kyle, you don't have to have sex with him, or even go out on a date with him, to build a relationship, that's what I'm saying. You like him, right?"

I nodded. "I do. More than I thought I would."

"Okay, time for another trip to Chemeketa. Let's find out what we can do to bring him out of that coma. It sounds like it might be time. Then you can try to make amends, and you need to eat crow and let him kick you in the ass if he needs to."

I sighed, finally coming to my senses. "Okay... you're right," I told her. "Even though I don't want you to be." She just chuckled and pushed me out the door.

I rushed home, showered, and packed. Lance and Drew said I could stay with them whenever I was in town. Lance was spending most nights with Katan any-way, trying to learn all he could about being the new mayor, and Drew said he would enjoy the company.

I was just about to leave when I felt the little ruby pendant my grandmother had left me calling from the bedroom. I seldom wore jewelry, but somehow this felt important, so I slipped the pendant around my neck like a necklace and headed out the door, hoping when I saw Conley again, he'd let me explain. *Damn, I really had fucked this up.*

TWELVE

CONLEY

Pain engulfed me while I slept, causing me to clutch my chest and curl into myself while I writhed on the ground. "Fuck!" I yelled, and could feel myself waking in real life.

I blinked as the room, filled with people, once again came into focus. "What... what happened?" I asked just as I noticed Kyle standing at the foot of the bed.

An older man standing to my right said, "We woke you." He looked toward Kyle, and I could see he hadn't been in agreement.

"Thank you. Oh, gods, this hurts," I said as I tried to lean up.

"No, don't try to sit up. The pain will subside as we work over you, but you'll need to be awake, and, if possible, chant with us as we try to heal you. We've done what we can for the physical wound, so we are going to work on the spiritual wound now."

I settled back down and felt them close the circle around me. I didn't know the chant, and the language was different, archaic, I thought. But before long, the rhythm and sounds came to my mind, and I was able to close my eyes and chant with them. At least when the pain was bearable.

Sweat beaded on my forehead as a cold fever lingered on the rest of my skin. I cried as the pain tore through me. How could anyone endure this? I was surely going to die.

Gradually, though, the pain subsided. Eventually, when all my energy was spent, I fell asleep. This time, there was no meadow, no dragons, and no handsome man waiting for me, just a dreamless, deep sleep.

THIRTEEN

KYLE

YVONNE EXPRESSED HER CONCERNS about the earthquake occurring in conjunction with the argument I'd had with Conley during the dream. "You know the darkness lurks. You can feel it. If we don't act, it could undo our very existence," she argued.

Both Rose and William Shepherd nodded sadly in agreement. "This will be excruciatingly painful," Rose said. "Although we've removed the poison, his heart still hasn't healed spiritually. We'll have to have a full quorum, no less than thirteen people." Rose shook her head. "We don't have enough Fire Guild members to do this, but I think with nine fire energies present, the rest can be filled by other elementals. Regardless, we'll have to work fast. It will be hard on him."

"Conley acknowledged he needed to wake," I said, and the couple left to round up the four other people we needed.

Rose contacted Lance and Katan and asked them to join us, then called Drew and a few other people that had to be brought into the loop. That completed our quorum, with a couple people to spare, in case they were needed.

The moment William recited the chant to wake Conley from the coma, I felt my grandmother's pendant heat up and the pain reignited in my own heart. I'd already figured that would happen, so I'd requested chairs be placed behind us, so I wouldn't put the circle at risk of being broken if I collapsed again.

The pain was momentous. At times I couldn't chant the words, but as I looked at poor Conley, I knew it was much worse for him. Finally, when he woke, William told him what was happening, and he acknowledged he wanted it, just as he'd told me. The chanting began again, and with it came the pain.

I knew when the healing had been completed; Conley fell into a deep and natural sleep, and my heart felt normal again. I was exhausted, and when the circle broke, Rose came over to where I stood next to Yvonne. "We've done all we can for him. He'll always have some scar tissue, and that could bring trouble in the future. His life may be cut short as a result, but for now, he will recover."

"Cut short? Like he'll die young? How long?" I asked, my heart now hurting in an entirely different way.

"We will assess that later when he wakes, but the damage was intense. He may only have a few years before his heart is unable to take the strain. I'm sorry," she said, and patted my hand before leaving.

"I didn't... I..."

Yvonne pulled me from the room. We sat in the Shepherds' living room, and Yvonne let me lean into her as tears I wasn't able to keep back slipped silently down my face. "This is my fault, isn't it? If I hadn't asked them to wake him…"

"Then we might all die. Honey, no, this isn't your fault. It was the cantation that struck him in the heart to begin with, so if anyone is to blame, it's your father."

I nodded. "But do you think he'd have longer to live if he'd stayed in the coma?" I asked, the guilt I felt threatening to swallow me whole.

"No, it's unlikely," I heard William say from behind me. "His wounds were deep and significant. The only reason he isn't dead is because the Kels kept him alive until we could get to him."

"So, there's nothing anyone can do to save him, to give him a longer life?"

William shrugged. "We aren't doctors, Kyle. But if you could get him medical help, here, what happens if he returns to his own dimension? How would he get and take the medications to keep him alive?" He shook his head as he spoke, and it was clear that he didn't think that particular course of action would work at all. "There are lots of decisions to make, and I'm afraid some will be difficult. But for now, if there's a threat to him, to you, or both our worlds because of the volcanic activity around us, that's what you should probably focus on. At worst, Conley, as you called him, will have several good years before his heart gives out. So those concerns aren't imminent."

I nodded, then asked, "When will he wake up?"

"Probably not until tomorrow. He's exhausted, as are you. Go and sleep," he said. "I'll let you know when he wakes."

Yvonne dropped me off at Drew and Lance's. "I've got to get back to Eugene, but I can come back to pick you up," she said before she left. "I don't think you'll need your car for a bit. Conley is going to need recovery time, then you can bring him back to Eugene with you, and he can stay with me if you aren't..."

"If he's willing, he can stay with me. But for now, yeah, I won't need my car. If I need to get around, I'll borrow Lance's."

She smiled and hugged me before she left. Drew welcomed me in and helped me carry my luggage to my old bedroom. Once again, it felt so strange to be back. My room had changed some since I'd left, but somehow being back here, in my grandmother's house, felt right, as if it was just what I needed. I ended up lying down and immediately falling asleep.

I instantly knew I was dreaming. Grandma stood next to me, the ever-present darkness at her back. "Hi, honey," she said when I opened my eyes.

"Hi, Grandma," I said, looking around the bedroom that now looked the same as when I'd moved in with her. I smiled at the posters of Josh Hartnett, Wentworth Miller, and Orlando Bloom hanging on my wall. I definitely had a type.

"He is recovering?" she asked.

I nodded. "But they said he won't live long, Grandma. What can we do?" I asked, and she shook her head.

"Not much, I'm afraid. The Shepherds would know, but for now, focus on the task at hand. The solutions to problems often come with the resolution of others."

"So you've said." I smiled at my grandma. "I-I like him, Grandma. I didn't mean to. I fought it, resisted it."

She nodded. "There's no requirement to marry him, Kyle. I should've made that clear. But, I'm... I'm just not myself any longer. I was stronger with your brothers, but my time has long past. I'm sorry."

I reached for her and was able to take her hand. "Grandma, it'll be over soon. I promise, then you can transition. I understand he and I are connected. I also understand I don't have to marry him. That's, um, I guess that's what I needed to hear. I needed to know I had a choice." I felt relief having confessed my feelings out loud, before the realization hit me that taking things further with Conley wouldn't be that simple. "Now, I just need to clean up the mess I made by deceiving him, then maybe he'll be able to forgive me."

She chuckled, the familiar gleam returning to her eyes. "Oh, honesty is always the best policy."

She kissed my forehead, and I saw the dark gathering behind her. She turned abruptly and thrust her hands out, causing air to flow out of her and toward Dad's cantation.

The darkness fought her, and I was alarmed as I noticed how she only just barely managed to keep it at bay.

When she saw I'd noticed, she sighed in frustration, then shook her head sadly. "I'm definitely getting weaker, but so is the cantation. I think that's why it's working to unbalance the dragons and Dóiteán. You can't let it do that. Trust Conley, I believe he can help you overcome the darkness, not just your father's cantation, but the darkness that's always desired to overthrow the light. Trust him," she said, then slowly disappeared.

Someone was shaking me gently, and I knuckled at my eyes.

"Kyle," my brother said. "Kyle, wake up. Do you want me to take you to the Shepherds' before I go to work?"

I sat up, trying to get my bearings. "Um, let me get a shower first, then I'll head over."

I probably should've rushed, but the dream had disturbed me. I felt especially concerned for my grandmother, whose spirit seemed to be languishing on this side of the veil. "Fuck you, Dad!" I said as the water from the shower sprayed on my face.

I descended the stairs and ran into Drew. "Hey, Lance had to speak with the council this morning, but said he'd be back to pick you up when they're done."

"Thanks, yeah, he told me. Is that coffee?" I asked, hoping my sense of smell was accurate.

"Yeah, I'll pour you a cup. What do you take in it?"

"Black is fine. I just need a little caffeine fortification to face everything today."

Drew poured the coffee and sat down across from me. "Wanna talk about it?" he asked.

For a moment, it felt like I was once again sitting across from my grandmother, getting advice from her. I guessed in a lot of ways, Drew was very much like her—patient and kind, but hard when he needed to be. The two of them had cared deeply for one another, and I trusted my grandmother's judgment of people. So, I decided to confide in him.

"Grandma showed up in my dreams. She doesn't look good, Drew. I mean, I know she's dead, but I've seen her spirit before, and she looked fine, strong even. Now she looks drawn, and my father's dark energy is lurking behind her. I don't think it lets her have a break."

Drew looked concerned. "Yeah." He waited a moment, staring into his coffee. "The reality is I used to be able to speak to her on a whim, but lately, I hesitate to reach out. I can tell every time I connect it takes something from her."

"Should we do something? Cast a protective spell to help her? Or something to help lift the veil for her?"

Drew shook his head. "No, it has to be her choice when she crosses. I'm still living, obviously, so I don't know all the secrets, but I know that much. But regarding whether or not we can protect her? Maybe. I'll ask the Kels if they know anything. Most of the ancestors who linger in the forest have been there for generations. There must be some secret to their longevity."

"Thanks," I said, and we both grew silent.

Finally, Drew got up and said he'd make us both some breakfast. "You may need it. Conley will need support and may even need to lean on you for more of your gifts. You're going to need fortitude for that," he said.

I ended up going out to the garden and walking along the narrow path that led to the stream that ran through the property. I could hear the tree frogs singing the moment I was under the forest canopy. It always surprised me, after being in more temperate climates, that the tree frogs continued to stay active during the winters in Oregon.

I was glad they did. Their songs always comforted me. I sat on a bench Lance and Crea had built by the stream with Dad. I'd still been really young, but I could remember the day like it was yesterday. Dad was so different then. He'd laughed at Crea's antics and embraced Lance, putting his arm around him, and pulling him close when the project was done. Then he'd scooped me up and placed me on the bench, proclaiming I should be the first to try it out.

My brothers had joined me shortly after that, and Dad had even taken a picture of us all sitting there together, proud as peacocks. A picture I hadn't seen in ages. How could a man go from being a loving father to who he was now? An evil dark spirit that had threatened and even tried to kill Lance, Crea, their lovers, and now me?

I felt the tears and didn't resist them. I'd never properly mourned the loss of our family. Part of me always felt it was because I'd been lucky to have our grandmother. Mom was always cold, and even as a young child, I felt she didn't like me very much. Grandma and Dad had been my world. Losing him had hurt. Lance's curse, the one he threw back at Dad that meant he'd never have our love again, had largely blocked my sadness for years, but maybe, because Crea and Lance had both done so much to break the curse, I was feeling the loss more powerfully now.

Maybe mourning was something we all needed. Maybe that was what this was all about, not just ending Dad's curse against us, but Lance's as well. We were all supportive of what Lance had said in the heat of the moment, but now? Was mourning the loss of our father the key to how these awful spells could be broken? I wish I knew the answer.

I stood to go back into the house, sensing Drew was done cooking. He smiled as I walked in, but we ate in silence. Somehow he must've known I was still in my head about my dad.

Lance showed up right after I'd brushed my teeth and was ready to go. "You okay?" he asked when I crawled into the passenger side.

"No," I said honestly. "Lance, the curse is less powerful. I can tell that, but this morning, I sat on the bench you, Crea, and Dad made all those years ago. I began feeling remorse and loss for the first time in... well, since that horrible night."

Lance nodded. "Yeah, I'm feeling a bit melancholy myself. Tell you what, why don't I find out when Crea and Eli are free? Maybe Jennie, too, and we can all get together here at Drew's, if he doesn't mind, and have a ceremony. We didn't attend Grandma's memorial service either, so it can be about all we've lost."

I nodded. "I'll... um, I'll ask Conley if he'd like to come too. I'm not sure why, but that feels important. Is that strange?"

"Maybe a little, but if it feels right and if he feels well enough to join us, that works for me."

Lance dropped me off at the Shepherds' house, and I was immediately met at the door by Conley. "Wow, you look so much better. I didn't expect..."

"Can we go for a walk?" Conley asked, interrupting me.

"Sure, as long as you feel up for it," I said, and turned toward the beach.

We walked in silence along the shore. He was wearing a leather jacket, which I assumed belonged to Philip, since it wasn't something I'd have expected him to bring with him from a mid-nineteenth century village in a different dimension. I was glad he had it, since it was still really chilly on the beach this time of year.

"I was really upset with you," Conley said without looking at me. "I told you stuff about me, because I thought you were my guide, my friend. I didn't... I wouldn't have shared all the stuff about my being, um, innocent if I'd known."

"Wait, Conley, look at me," I said.

He stopped and turned toward me, and my stomach dropped at the hurt expression on his face. "First, I'm not judging you because you haven't fooled around with another guy. Trust me, when you do, it'll all come naturally. Well, most of it will. You'll figure out the rest as time goes on. I didn't tell you the truth, because I didn't want to feel trapped. I wanted to maintain my right to make my own decisions... to not be dictated to. Like that arranged marriage you mentioned. I don't want that for myself."

"And you couldn't have just said that?" he asked. I could tell he was still pissed at me, not that I could blame him.

"Yeah, I could've, and I should've. But, in my defense, I didn't really know you. Just the concept of you. We didn't become friends until we'd spent time together. I don't want to make you angrier, but can I be totally honest?" I asked.

He nodded yes, but I could sense his hesitation.

"I think we got closer, became friends even, because we weren't tied to relationship rules set out by other people. Was it unfair and even unscrupulous that I kept it a secret about who I was in all this? Yeah, but faced with the same choice, I'd do it again." When he narrowed his eyes at me, I continued, "I'd do it again, because now, I like you because I like you, not because I'm supposed to, or worse, destined to."

He didn't respond for several moments, before he asked, "But you do *like* me?"

I grabbed hold of his hand and drew him against me. "I *like* you... a lot," I admitted, and almost smiled as he allowed me to kiss him.

He was so eager, so willing, that I wished we were somewhere private, so I could show him just how much I liked him. Considering he was new to all this, though, I also didn't want to rush. We could just enjoy each other's company instead of me pushing things too fast for him.

We walked way down the beach until we almost made it to the state park. "You must really be feeling better," I said, "...considering how far we've walked. Do you have any pain in your chest or shortness of breath?"

He shook his head. "No. Mr. Shepherd told me I have permanent heart damage, and I'll have issues as time goes on, but I woke up feeling good. Better than good, if I'm honest."

"The Fire Guild folks have been working round the clock sending you energy and working to improve your condition. Speaking of that, I'm really sorry about having to wake you up early. I felt the pain you were experiencing yesterday. It was intense."

"Worst thing I've ever endured," Conley said. We were still holding hands, and he gave mine a little squeeze. "I thought I was going to pass out more than once. Just so we're clear, I *do not* like your dad."

That made me chuckle, and it felt good to hear his sense of humor had returned. "That would make two of us. In fact, there are a lot of people who'd agree with you right about now."

Fourteen

Conley

I'D WOKEN UP EARLY that morning before anyone else in the house had gotten up. The pain I'd felt the day before was completely gone, and I felt extremely rested, but I remained in bed, thinking about Kyle and our predicament.

I'd already decided to forgive him, although not before I told him how I felt, but I also understood it. No one wanted to be forced into a relationship, and sure as hell not with someone like me.

All of my self-esteem baggage aside, he'd told me he liked me, and he'd told me about the curse his dad had placed on him and his brothers. It was no surprise he wanted to push his destiny away. Hell, I'd felt the exact same way when the dragons and the ancestors had tried to convince me to go on this quest.

Until now, I hadn't found anyone I wanted to be with, not in any way, be it friend or lover. Now, I was ex-pected to take on this stranger, and with no question about whether I liked him or not? Yeah, I could totally understand why he'd lied.

That didn't mean I didn't feel betrayed, though. Kyle and I had spent a lot more time together than had actually passed in his world. Unlike how I'd lost an entire year in real life while I'd been with the ancestors and dragons in my vision, what felt like months of getting to know each other while in the dream state was in truth not the case at all.

Mrs. Shepherd had told me this morning after inviting me to breakfast that it'd actually only been a few weeks. The whole time-slippage thing was ridiculously confusing, but it did little to diminish my feelings for Kyle.

I'd felt his arrival, and since I was sitting alone in the Shepherds' sitting room looking at a book they had on their coffee table, I didn't hesitate to jump up and open the door to greet him. I didn't want our conversation to be here, at a stranger's house. I wanted it to be just us, like it'd been in the meadow.

When he kissed me, well, that had felt so good. I was afraid maybe being upset would've turned him off, but if that kiss was any indication, he wasn't, not that I was any judge of that. I'd only kissed one other person, a boy from another village I'd met when I was twenty. His family was traveling through and wanted to use the portal back to Earth. Of course, when they crossed back over, the guy acted as though he'd never seen me before.

Kyle was different, I could tell he was different, and I wanted to do so much more than just kiss him. I wanted to explore him in every way possible.

We ended up walking for miles, which for some reason felt right for my body. It was hungry for exercise.

"So, you know about the predicament with your heart?" Kyle asked as we walked hand in hand back toward the Shepherds' house.

"Yeah, I know it's ominous, but I think our healers may possess more advanced powers than yours in this dimension. Being so close to the veil, we have a different approach to life and death."

Kyle was silent after that. We were almost back where we started, when he said, "My grandmother, I saw her in a vision today. She looked... she didn't look good, Conley. Is there anything you can do for her, anything that can be done on that side of the portal? I'm really concerned."

I thought for a moment before responding. "Me? No. But there are plenty of people who specialize in healing energies in Dóiteán. Often the spirit is the most difficult part of the healing process, so there are experts in just that."

"Can your healers possibly heal a curse?"

Again, I shrugged. "I mean, you know my training was for leadership. The guilds in Dóiteán each have a different focus. All I can do is advise you on who to ask. Think of me as a resource, like the big books kept in libraries."

"Or Google," he said, completely confusing me.

"Who is Google?" I asked, and he chuckled.

"It's a computer thing. Think of it as an information portal. I'll show you later. For now, I have an idea, a weird idea, and one that's probably way far-fetched, but it's a place to start. Would you be willing to join my brothers and me for a ceremony to acknowledge the loss of our grandmother, and allow ourselves to mourn the loss of our father? I'm beginning to think that's the next path to ending the curse for good."

I nodded and smiled at the hope I saw in Kyle's face. "Yes, I'm happy to help any way I can. Meanwhile, I'd like to kiss you again, is that okay?"

Kyle smiled, the seriousness abandoning his features in a delightful way. "I'd like that very, very much!"

Fifteen

— · —

Kyle

I SPENT THE WEEK with Conley, and had no words to express how much I enjoyed it. Like when we'd been in the meadow, he was funny, often saying things to deliberately get me to laugh. He was also charming, although I didn't think that was deliberate on his part. On the other hand, I could tell he had low self-esteem, which made absolutely no sense. The man was perfect in so many ways.

Crea, our niece Jennie, and Eli were all scheduled to return home in the middle of the following week. Eli had accepted a commission in Toronto, and was traveling back and forth with Jennie, who he'd taken as his apprentice, while the museum that'd commissioned the work communicated what they wanted. Crea, I'd just learned, was taking over the community gardens in Chemeketa, and didn't have much work to do until spring, so he'd been traveling with them.

I was still finding everything that had happened–Crea and Lance both finding love, let alone moving back to Chemeketa and becoming involved in the communi-ty–bewildering. It made sense, especially with this new feeling of mourning coming over me and even Lance and Crea, who'd told me he'd been having the same melancholy feelings Lance had mentioned earlier, that the curses were weakening. That could only be a good thing.

What was missing was alone time with Conley. If I'd had my car, I might've driven us back to Eugene, where we could've had some privacy, but Yvonne was buried with work regarding the recent earthquake. She wasn't free to just drop everything and come pick me up, and Lance needed his car. I guess I could've rented one, but just up and leaving town right now didn't feel right either.

One thing that did work out was a visit to the Kels. Crea and Eli were moving into a house on the top of an extinct volcano located in the great woods. Edward Edenfield, the leader of the Kels and head of the Air Guild in Chemeketa, met us there, explaining that the Kels preferred not to leave the forest unless absolutely necessary.

"The ancestors are able to remain fortified and strong because they're mostly confined to the boundaries of the great forest," he told us. "We want them to continue to remain in this dimension for as long as they wish, so we do what we can to protect them, and strengthen them while they are here."

"Can that be done for our grandmother?" I asked.

Edward nodded, but looked skeptical. "I knew your grandmother Gwen. She was a free spirit, and I can't imagine binding her to Chemeketa would be her wish. Besides, if she was bound here, in this dimension, she wouldn't be able to travel back and forth between

Dóiteán and here. We..." he said, making a sweeping hand gesture indicating the Kels, "...have all felt her move through the portal, as if she were mortal. There must be a reason why she is moving between the dimensions."

I nodded and looked over at Conley, who hadn't spoken since our conversation with the Kel leader had begun. "So, unless we bind her to this dimension, to the boundaries of Chemeketa or some other place, we can't fortify her spirit?" I asked.

Edward thought for several moments, before he said, "There is one other option, one that might be better for her." He looked directly at Conley. "The dimension between Earth and the veil, where you live, doesn't require the same energy to communicate with spirits. Mostly, and this is just theoretical, our people believe that dimension has always existed as a go-between for the living and the deceased. I'd say it may be better, especially if you're concerned about Gwen, to communicate with her there, in that dimension."

I had already thought something similar, though I wasn't sure if that was because I really thought it would help my grandmother or I wanted to see the real Dóiteán, not just the version in my dreams. Hearing Edward confirm my suspicions helped.

"So, shall we try that?" I asked and glanced at Conley.

He smiled. "I've had no direction from the dragons or ancestors whether we should be here or in Dóiteán, just that we should work together to return the balance. Besides, the lands around Dóiteán are much wilder than here. More like the great forest. It could be fun to show you my favorite spots."

I couldn't help but smile in return. I knew he was saying we could have more alone time there than we did here. "So, that settles it then. After we hold the ceremony with my brothers, I'll follow you back to Dóiteán, and we will do what we can to overcome this stupid curse once and for all."

Sixteen

Conley

THE NIGHT THE BROTHERS celebrated the life of their grandmother was beautiful. Crea, Eli, and Jennie, as well as Jennie's girlfriend Scarlett, joined hands first.

"We bring the earth to this special occasion. Catch the scent of our grandmother's passion."

A feeling of happiness, a glow of green light, flowed up from the earth, filling each of us. Then, flowers of every imaginable kind began to sprout from the ground. You could tell they were just an illusion of magic, but that made them no less beautiful.

Next, Lance and Drew joined the circle.

"Light as air and thick as ice, we share our love from our grandmother's life. We cast up these earthen scents to embolden Gwen Franklyn's sight."

A breeze flowed in from the ocean and engulfed us. The smell of the sea blended with the scents of the flowers and their heady fragrance made me feel light and carefree.

Kyle took my hand then, leading me to the circle, where we joined the group around the fire pit. Neither of us had prepared anything, but I instinctively knew what he was going to say. I didn't join his chant, but lent my energy to him.

"Light is light, and night is night, through fire we bring the spirit right."

I felt the energy pulled from me, a great burst of it, enough to cause me to look at Kyle, whose face had taken on a glow.

"Seek the peace and balance forth, our grandmother's will shall be our course!"

The fire burst upward into the sky, heat enveloping us all before we could shy away from it. When it died down, in the fire pit stood the old woman I'd seen in my dreams. Gwen Franklyn. Suddenly, I understood. *She* was the guide the dragons and ancestors had mentioned. She smiled as she stepped from the pit. The fire had been replaced by her spirit. She went to each person in the circle, appearing to bless each one as she greeted them.

She didn't speak out loud, maybe she couldn't, but I could tell she was here because we had all lent our energy to her. As she blessed each person, I witnessed them each as emotions overcame them. They were each saying goodbye to her.

When she came to Kyle and me, she smiled, but it was sad. *"You have much yet to endure,"* I heard her say in my head. *"I'm stronger because of you, and because of our family, but your journey has just begun."*

Sweet and loving energy flowed through me as she blessed us and what we had together, although it was new and undefined. Then she returned to the pit. As she disappeared, her image was replaced by fire once more.

We stood silently before Kyle, Crea, and Lance broke the circle and stepped forward, joining hands around the pit.

"Blood to blood, we seek our father, so he may know we have felt great sorrow. Tonight, we cleanse the darkness away and forgive the betrayal he sent our way."

Where Gwen had stood moments before, love emanating from her, now there was anger. Darkness rose behind us, and its malicious intent was clear. Its single desire was to destroy us.

At once, Lance, Crea, and Kyle must've been hit with similar attacks, because they all cried out in pain at the same time. As they were recovering, but before they could react, a light—small at first, but there nonetheless—drew up from the center of the fire pit. And as it grew, spiritual tattoos of precious stones began to shine on Crea and Eli's hands, and on the foreheads of Lance and Drew.

Power began to flow from the tattoos into the light, which grew stronger. Eventually, the light burst forth from the fire pit and into the darkness, scattering it.

When the burst of light faded, the three brothers were weeping. "It's done," Lance said. "The curse I cast on our father has been broken."

"Now what?" Kyle asked.

"Now, we mourn," Crea said.

The three brothers embraced as the tears flowed. Eli, Jennie, Scarlett, and Drew took my hand, and we created a small circle around them, and sent our energy into their healing.

I didn't know the full story behind the curse, only speculation and whispers from the Fire Guild folks who'd stuck around to visit with me after the healing. However, I knew something powerful had happened that night. I was so blessed to be part of something that freed these three men. Not only for my own healing regarding my family, but also to be a part of it for a man I'd begun to feel close to, my friend and maybe even my true soulmate.

***

Along with Crea and Eli, we spent the night with Drew and Lance. Kyle was emotionally spent, and I could feel his need to be held. So, when he asked me to stay, I wanted nothing more than to do just that.

I held him as he wept in my arms. As he slept, I could almost see the dark oily energy flow out of him and drain into the fire pit, where the coals that still burned devoured the hate and anger and turned it into pure light and energy that would no longer feed the darkness that had surrounded us earlier.

The next morning, there was a lightness to the brothers I hadn't noticed before. They laughed and teased one another in a way that I thought shocked them. The darkness that I'd seen spiritually leaving Kyle must've left them too, giving them a sense of peace they probably hadn't felt in a while.

Later, as Kyle and I took a stroll together, hand in hand along the beach, Kyle told me the story of his family. How his father had cursed them never to find love, then how Lance had cursed their father back, a curse he and Crea had strengthened with their own anger and feelings of betrayal.

"So, that's what was extinguished last night?" I asked, although I already knew the answer.

"Yes," Kyle said thoughtfully. "We released our anger and hatred toward our father, and our mother, too, for everything that she did and didn't do."

"How do you feel?" I asked.

"Better, lighter, but also sad." He leaned into me as we walked. "I'm so thankful you stayed with me last night. I'm not sure why, but having someone to hold..."

He didn't finish the statement, but I knew what he meant. "You're welcome, but..." I said, and stopped walking until Kyle halted and looked back at me. "I want more than holding and cuddling. I know that's what you needed last night, and it's what I wanted too, but even though I'm inexperienced... I *want* you, Kyle."

I blushed at my own forwardness. I'd never been so bold with a man before, and despite my confident words, I think Kyle saw through them.

I grabbed his shirt and pulled him into a kiss that sent fire into my belly, then down into my groin. He wrapped his arms around me until our bodies were pressed tight, so tight I could feel his interest. "Soon," he said, giving me a quick squeeze before he stepped away. Then, he grinned at me for a moment, before sprinting down the beach.

It took me a moment longer to recover, but when I did, I chased him. Feeling almost like a caveman chasing down his man, the need to take him, love him, was overwhelming. I knew the time was coming soon that I would.

Seventeen

Kyle

ENERGY. IT WAS SUCH a strange thing. As a volcanologist, I understood the power of how the simplest things, even something as ordinary as water vapor, could completely blow a mountain apart.

Anger and hatred were powerful too. Maybe more than my brothers, I'd held onto that hatred like a baby clutching its blanket. It'd been me who'd caused my brothers to come out to our parents, so when it all went horribly bad, I'd internalized it all.

I could remember the events of that day so clearly, of pouring my anger into Lance as he cast his spell. It was a visceral anger, the depth of which I'd never felt before or since, and I was sure my pubescent self only added to the fire I already had inside me.

As my brothers and I had gathered around the fire pit, the moment the light appeared, I knew what it meant. I was ashamed to say, at first, I didn't really want to let it go. If I surrendered the anger I still felt for both my parents' betrayal that day, what would I have left?

Grandma had known, though. She must've seen what was going to happen, because during the blessing, she'd said, *"You will have to let go of the past if you want to embrace your future."* She'd kissed my forehead, and although I couldn't feel her touch physically, my spirit recognized the feeling, and my heart's energy grew with the love I'd always felt for that amazing woman—a woman who not only saved my brothers and me, but who'd loved us unconditionally, something our parents weren't able to do.

When it was my turn to give up the anger–but not forgive, and never forget–the light exploded like a starburst in the sky, and the darkness that'd gathered around us retreated.

That was an important part of overcoming the darkness, and by allowing myself to let go, I was filled with love and joy I hadn't felt since my childhood.

Conley had spent the night holding me as my body expelled the anger and hurt. I could feel it flowing out of me, light replacing the darkness, and with it came emotions too big for me to handle on my own.

Although my time with Conley only amounted to a few weeks in real life, in the spiritual realm, we'd spent months together. I was beginning to feel a lot more than just friendship for him. I wanted him sexually, and I'd said as much, but wanting him as a partner or mate? That was not something I'd fully understood or even felt, until that night I fell asleep in his arms.

When Conley pulled me to him and kissed me, admitting he wanted me too, I almost broke down. So, like a coward, I literally ran away.

Luckily, it became a game, and Conley chased me along the beach, both of us laughing as we played.

The time slipped away, and it was much later when we got back to Drew and Lance's place. It seemed strange no longer thinking of it as Grandma's house, or even my place too, but they'd made it their own. Lance and Drew clearly belonged together, so did Crea and Eli, for that matter. I just hadn't been able to see it until now, not until the darkness was purged from my soul.

Okay, enough of the weirdo emotions. Gods, what next? Am I gonna start writing sappy romance novels or something?

I chuckled as Conley slipped his arm around my waist as I realized I really did like him that much. I could totally write a mushy romance novel about how much, and all the lovely things I wanted to do with him to show just how much.

That night, as Conley lay in my arms, things began to move toward more. Our kisses, gentle at first, stirred deeper feelings, and everything I'd felt during our carefree day together began to pour out of me.

I crawled on top of him, kissing his neck, letting my tongue trace up the shell of his ear, before whispering my admission, "I want you so much, Conley."

Just as I was about to show him, lightning struck outside the house, literally knocking me off Conley and onto the floor, then another bolt struck close to the house, and this time, I saw it for what it was. This wasn't natural lightning, it was dark, filled with rage and anger.

"Guys!" I yelled, before slipping a t-shirt on and running out of the bedroom in my underwear.

Conley was up and following me as we rushed to find Drew and Lance.

"What's going on?" Drew asked from their bedroom doorway.

"Did you not feel that?" I asked as another bolt of lightning struck just outside.

Lance came up behind Drew, and both men shook their heads. "No, feel what?"

"Shit," I said, and looked at Conley. "You felt it, right?"

His eyes were the size of saucers. "Yeah," he said as he nodded.

"Lightning, black lightning. It struck so close, it knocked me out of bed," I said, not mentioning that I was about to make love to my boyfriend for the first time. *Boyfriend?* I'd have to contemplate that later.

Drew rushed to the living room and set out a white candle. "Come stand with me," he said, and when we were all gathered around, he lit it.

"Light the wards of the forces that be, protect this home from the power I don't see. Surround this home with our energy's shower, so the dark may not enter the wards we empower."

It felt as though locks were sealing shut around us, and just in time, too, as another bolt of the dark lightning struck, but this time I didn't feel it. "That was scary," Conley whispered beside me, and I slipped my hand in his.

"Yeah, it seemed more powerful, and you didn't feel it?" I asked my brother, then looked to Drew.

Both of them shook their heads.

"How is that possible? What's going on?" I asked.

Drew sighed. "I'd normally call Gwen, but she's not really able to be on this plane of existence any longer since she said goodbye last night. But I sense you need her. I'm not sure what to do."

He might not have been sure, but I suddenly was. "I think we need to go back to Dóiteán. Grandma can exist easier there since it's closer to the veil."

Drew nodded. "You should probably go as soon as possible. I can't protect you like this..." he said, waving his hand around the room, "...for long. It worked this time, but my wards aren't designed to protect against this kind of assault. In fact, you should know, when Lance and I started dating, the darkness tried to kill me, almost did. If it wasn't for Alegia, Scarlett, and the Kels, it probably would've."

I nodded. "Okay. Conley, we should return to your dimension, and soon. Tomorrow, perhaps?"

"I think that's what we were always supposed to do," he said. "The dragons will protect us there, as well as your grandmother. I've seen her there, and she is stronger."

"Then, it's settled. We leave for Dóiteán in the morning."

EIGHTEEN

CONLEY

STRANGELY, WHILE I'D BARELY explored this dimension, it felt good to be going home. When preparing for my quest, I'd thought I'd get to visit one of their cinemas, or shop in one of the huge markets filled with goods from all over the world, just like in the stories Langley, who'd gone through the portal frequently, told us about.

Instead, I spent most of my time in a coma, and more recently, wandering the village of Chemeketa with Kyle. Not that I minded. It was still different here than in Dóiteán. Just seeing the air and earth energies in action was amazing. Most of the people in Dóiteán channeled fire energies. We had a few who weren't, of course, kids who'd been born with other gifts, or if someone had crossed the portal with a spouse that wasn't fire energy. But, for the most part, we were there to help keep the dragons from... well, from exploding.

I was excited to show Kyle my home. I was eager to spend time with him in the real meadow, the place I'd grown to love as my getaway, maybe even wade in the cold river now that spring was warming the water.

By now, the birds would be building their nests, and the migrating creatures would be returning to our part of the world. Spring had always been my favorite time of year.

Of course, spring was a big deal for all of Dóiteán. On the equinox––a time when the fire energies were at their strongest–we'd have a huge celebration as we brought in the return of the sun coming to full strength. Even the dragons couldn't compete with the fire power of the sun. Yes, it was time to go home.

We left after breakfast. Drew had cooked, something I could tell he enjoyed doing. I allowed myself to think of a time when maybe I would be cooking for Kyle. Maybe even a time when Kyle's family were in Dóiteán to visit.

"You should plan to visit Dóiteán, all of you," I said on impulse, and when I turned toward Kyle, he was smiling.

"You want my family to come to Dóiteán?" he asked.

I blushed. "Well, yeah, we don't have many visitors, but the portal is open to anyone who feels drawn to our village. We've never kept people out."

Drew smiled. "I think that'd be nice. I'd enjoy seeing your home and seeing Gwen, too, if she is indeed strong enough to visit us there."

"I'll send word with Langley, he's our traveler between the dimensions. I'll let you know when things have cooled off enough with all this," I said, waving toward the front of the house where the lightning had struck last night.

Drew looked concerned. "Just don't expect it to be fast or easy," he said. "The darkness is weaker than it was with us, but it's still very dangerous. You must never underestimate it."

I nodded, feeling just a bit chastised. "I understand, but we have to maintain hope, don't we? If we give in to fear, we lose before we start."

"Well said," Lance responded as he came around me and patted my back. "But, Drew's right. You should know it's a terrible thing that'll destroy you if it can. I learned that the hard way when I tried to ignore it."

Drew chuckled and cringed at the same time. "It was ugly," he said.

"Don't let your fear of it keep you from living, but you should keep your eye on it as well. You can be safe and live. It's a balance."

I took their words to heart, and we left shortly after. "I like your family," I said as we moved into the forest.

"Yeah, to my surprise, I do too."

He shrugged when I looked confused. "I think maybe the curse against our father blocked our love for each other. It's kept us apart. Now it's extinguished, it's like I feel more for them..." He pondered for a moment. "I think we can feel our love for each other in a way we weren't able to before."

I nodded. "You've freed yourself."

I stopped at the cave entrance just as the Kel spirits began to gather around us. I bowed to them before walking in, thanking them for guarding us. I could feel the portal as we got closer. It was different from the time I'd entered from the other side.

I felt it in my heart, the place where I'd been stabbed. Absently, I reached up and rubbed my chest. Kyle noticed and asked if I was okay.

"Yeah, just bad memories of the last time I was here," I said, and Kyle drew me to him and kissed me.

"When we're in Dóiteán, the first thing on the agenda is to have your healers look at that, okay?"

I nodded, took Kyle's hand, and we walked into the portal together.

Nineteen

Kyle

THE MOMENT THE ENERGY shifted around us, I knew I'd made a mistake. Pain radiated out from my chest, and I realized I hadn't put up any shields to protect either me or Conley. You'd think after what'd happened to Conley upon entering into Chemeketa, we'd have learned.

I crumbled to the ground, clutching my chest that now felt like someone was trying to rip my heart out with their bare hands.

I looked up and saw the darkness, the way it looked at the meadow, swirling around me. "I'm going to die," I whispered.

Then, I heard Conley chanting next to me, but I couldn't make out what he was saying. I squeezed my eyes shut, trying to reduce some of the pain, before my chest slowly began to loosen. Eventually, I was able to stand.

"Sorry," I said when I could catch my breath. "I should've been prepared."

Conley was still chanting under his breath as he led me out of the cave on the other side. His side. We had reached his home. I could see the three dragons flying toward us, and as soon as they were overhead, the pain eased even more. "Damn," I said as Conley let me slide down to the ground.

He knelt beside me. "I'm sorry too. I should've known that would happen."

"We both should've. It's not like Drew and Lance didn't warn us this morning."

Conley sighed next to me. "Okay, so from now on, we take this more seriously. We're at war with your dad's curse or cantation, or whatever you call it. We should never go anywhere without being on guard."

"Agreed. Now, our first step should be seeing those healers you spoke of," I said. "For both of us."

The hike from the cave to the village was a pretty arduous one. Fortunately, it was mostly downhill, so that helped. By the time we stumbled into the village, I thought I'd gone as far as I could. Had it not been for Conley's patience and support, I'd have never made it. I'd suffered no physical wound like Conley when he had been attacked–I assumed his chanting over me helped prevent further injury–but I was still in excruciating pain. Something serious had happened to me, and I knew I needed help.

The moment people recognized Conley, they rushed forward to express how good it was to see him. I could tell he was a bit surprised by their reaction. "Absence makes the heart grow fonder?" I asked quietly, so only he could hear.

"Apparently," he whispered back. We didn't stop to talk to anyone as we slowly made out way further into the village.

"I need the healers," he yelled out when we came around a corner into the village square.

He sat me down on a bench facing a beautiful fountain that spat fire instead of water. "Well, that's different," I said as Conley looked toward the fountain.

"Fire energy," he said, and chuckled. "We know how to express it to its fullest here."

I stared into the flames a moment before noticing a woman in a long dark robe rushing toward me. "I'm Doctor Gonzales, the medico here," she said. "Let me take a look at you." I probably shouldn't have been surprised to hear a Mexican Spanish accent, one very similar to that of the villagers around Popocatépetl. Conley had already told me Dóiteán was diverse.

"What hurts? What happened?" she asked Conley.

I listened as Conley explained. Then, to my surprise, the doctor pulled out a stethoscope and listened to my heart. I assumed medical care would be more magic-based, not like home. "I don't believe it's physical, so that's something," she said. She turned to a young boy who'd followed her here. I could tell by the resemblance, he must be her son. "Go get Guha Cho, tell him we have an emergency. I'm taking this man to the clinic. Have him meet us there," Dr. Gonzales said.

Whoever Guha Cho was, he arrived at the clinic the same time we did. I was once again surprised to see a modern-looking facility. *Time to stop assuming*, I thought, just as another wave of pain shot through my heart, making me grab my chest and struggle to breathe.

I heard Conley explain his attack and then mine as he speedily caught the two up on what had happened to us.

"His heart is beating fine, but from what Conley is saying, it makes sense," Dr. Gonzales said. "His heart was attacked physically on Earth, but this man would be more susceptible to spiritual attack here. This is more along your line of treatment, señor Cho."

"I agree," the man next to her said. "I'll examine him while you do the same with Conley. I'm guessing the two are connected."

The man leaned me back onto a bed, similar to those in our doctor's offices, and said, "I'm going to cast a spell over you now, mostly to have you rest. Then, I'll examine you. You'll be awake, but drowsy. Do you understand?"

I nodded, and with the pain building, I wasn't going to argue about anything he wanted to do, especially if it helped me feel better.

He waved his hands over my face, then above my head before moving his hovering hands up and down my body. I could feel the energy radiating from him. Wherever his hands moved, my body felt warmth, followed by an intense feeling of relaxation.

Right before I fell asleep, he stopped and smiled down at me. "That should make you feel better. I'm going to look at your heart now. This could hurt, but I want to see what's happening more than deal with it, so if you feel pain, please let me know."

I nodded sleepily. He closed his eyes, and I felt more than saw his spirit separate from his body. Then, I began to feel his hands moving across my rib cage. His fingers probed my chest, then I felt him touch something, something that felt as if it was protruding from me.

When I cried out in pain, Mr. Cho's spirit came back to him. "It's serious," he said. "You'll need more than me to heal this."

I reached for him before he could leave. "When Conley crossed over into our world, he was physically attacked. A barb struck him in his heart," I said, and even though I was so tired, I forced myself to continue. "The people called the Kels were able to save him, stop the bleeding, but if there's a barb in me, it's similar. I just wanted you to understand."

"I do," Mr. Cho said. "Were you there when they healed him?"

"Yes, I was there."

"You are linked. Rest now. I'll do what's needed to remove the spiritual barb," he said, and waved his hand over my face. This time, I fell into a dreamless sleep.

Twenty

Conley

Mr. Cho frowned at me as he explained what had to be done. "You should've warded yourself. What have I been teaching you?"

I looked down, shame coursing through me. It was just like being in fifth-grade special-powers class again. I'd sucked at remembering things then, and apparently, that hadn't changed.

"You'll need to be the one who leads the circle," he said. "From what it looks like, the barb that was in you is the physical manifestation of the spiritual one in him."

He went about putting together items for the spell we'd be casting. "You know this was a delay tactic. It wanted to kill you, of course, but it must have known that wasn't your destiny. This is to delay the work you're supposed to be doing together."

"And what is that?" I asked, hoping maybe my old mentor and our community's spiritual leader might have more insight than me.

"I'm not sure. I tried scrying when you went missing, and again when you returned, but the fire crystal I used literally turned brown. I had to cleanse it in my stove for a week, and it's still not right."

"That's pretty much how I've felt too," I admitted. "I have no idea what I'm doing. The dragons aren't much help. The most I've gotten from them is to fall in love with this man. Shouldn't there be more to it than that?"

He shrugged and added rosemary to the herbs he was mixing. "If you want my honest opinion, I think that's just part of it. Your destiny is more than I think any of us are able to see. If it helps, I think it's good for you and this man... Kyle is his name, right?" I nodded. "I think you should just show Kyle around, get to know him better, and see where things lead, then the answers will come."

"You know how much I like ambiguity," I said sarcastically, causing the old man to chuckle.

It felt like old times as I helped Mr. Cho add herbs to the boiling water in the old cauldron hanging over his fireplace. Of course, he also had a modern gas range like all the residents used. The natural gas well we found thirty miles from our village provided a modern way of cooking, while still supporting our fire energy ways.

But for spells and potions, most Dóiteán residents preferred the old ways. Well, the older folks did. I honestly never had a good hand with spellcasting myself. I wasn't very good at anything, if I was honest. And there was the rub. I should've been one of the more gifted practitioners here, or at least that was what my mother and grandmother had repeatedly told me. Instead, I'd put myself and Kyle in danger because I'd never been gifted with the sense my ancestors possessed.

"Your father is descended from the first witch to cross this boundary. Our mothers and grandmothers were powerful witches in India before we felt the call to come here. Why are you lacking such power?" they'd asked. I had no answers then, and I had none now.

Once the potion was complete, Mr. Cho helped me undress Kyle from the waist up, then left as I spread the potion over his chest. "You'll need to sing to him," he said. I knew his request came from my total inability to rhyme. I sucked at chanting. But, I could sing, at least enough to call upon the magic within me. As limited as that might be.

"Come to me. Your soul is light. I will be your shining knight."

The words flowed from me. Always nonsense words, but I could feel their power, pulling from the depths of me.

"Cast out this barb that holds you down. And let me be your lover bound."

I hummed as my intense concentration began to give way to the hypnotic state I always went into when working with magic.

All the while, I continued running my hands over Kyle's muscular torso. His pecs were firm, and his stomach was flat, unlike the tiny bit of pudge I tended to carry around my middle. Even in a magical trance, I could see how attractive he was. I noticed the line of hair that started at his navel and trailed down below his jeans, and I immediately felt the red dragon's presence.

She didn't speak, didn't do anything. It was as if she existed inside me, and her highly sexualized character had heightened to its maximum.

I poured the potion over his abdomen and hummed, pulling power from the red dragon herself as I massaged the magic into his body. As I rubbed it into his skin, I could feel pouring myself and the dragon into his soul.

I wasn't sure when I ran out of potion, or when I blinked out, but I woke up standing on the red dragon's mountaintop.

"You want him," I heard Dearg say. It wasn't a question.

I nodded, but didn't respond.

"Then you should take him. Lead him to the cabin in the woods at the base of my mountain. Bring him and live with him there. Let your bodies learn to be together."

"He's injured," I said sadly, wanting more than anything to take the red dragon up on her offer.

"The injury isn't permanent, and is better fought when you're together. Let the healers remove the barb, then bring him to my mountain and help him recover here."

I woke up sitting in a chair across from Kyle. He was awake and looking at me with hunger in his eyes, the kind of hunger I'd felt when I was applying the potion to his body. "I was there," he said. "On the mountain with the dragon."

"Do you want to go? Do you want to be with me there?" I asked.

He nodded slowly, his gaze trailing down my body as he licked his lips. In that moment, I knew we were about to become much more for one another than we'd been until now.

Twenty-One

Kyle

I HOPED WE'D BE on our way to the cabin soon, but that wasn't the case. The barb took more than just a quick spell or spiritual tug to remove. In fact, a week passed before the spiritual leader, Guha Cho, was able to completely remove it.

Then, there was a week of recovery while he and the healers removed the dark stains on my heart. Meanwhile, I was unable to get my hands on Conley. We were clearly being cockblocked by the darkness.

Frustrated, I wanted to lash out, but these people had been good to me. I couldn't take my frustrations out on them.

"You are Kyle Franklyn?" a tiny woman, no more than four and a half feet tall, asked one afternoon after I woke from a nap.

I turned to her and smiled. "Yes, and you are?"

"I'm Conley's mother, Aine."

I sat up, although it was still a bit painful to do so. "It's a pleasure to meet you, Mrs. Bolcan," I said, and reached out my hand.

She smiled, which was nice to see as she'd been frowning up until then. "You will have dinner with us tonight. My husband and I would like to greet you properly and get to know you better," she said, and turned to go.

It was a summons, not an invitation, and from her expression when she'd first announced herself, I was pretty sure she wasn't happy I existed. I had several friends and colleagues whose families had moved to the US from India, and I knew from those friendships, Indian moms could be quite rigid when it came to their children's relationships. I needed to tread lightly for both my and Conley's sake.

Despite the residual pain, I got up and showered to make myself presentable. I smiled when I saw clean clothes on the table. I assumed Mr. Cho had put them out for me while I'd slept, knowing Conley's mother was going to make an appearance.

I also assumed since the clothing was there, he approved of my going. I was not sure how I felt about it. I was even less sure how Conley would feel, but I'd been summoned, so I would go.

Even such simple things as showering and dressing took it out of me. My energy levels were still low, and I was dreading the walk across the village to where Conley lived.

The clothes I had been given to wear were so different from anything I'd seen before. They were like a mix between traditional Indian garments and something verging on Victorian. Also, the silk was different. It glowed as I rubbed my hand across it. Blues and greens, which, to be honest, were the colors that looked best on me.

I looked in the mirror, pleased that I didn't look too bad, even if my complexion was several shades lighter than it normally was, and I appeared exhausted. Okay, now to find someone who could tell me how the hell to get to Conley's home.

I walked down the stairs of the clinic, having to stop at the bottom to catch my breath. When I opened the main door and stepped outside, Conley was waiting there with a man I instantly knew had to be his father. You couldn't mistake the strong features and high noble cheekbones in both faces.

They were sitting in some kind of open carriage, not unlike the first cars made in my dimension. There was no horse, so I assumed it had an engine, or maybe even ran on magic.

"Hey, you should've waited," Conley said as he jumped out and rushed to help me. The moment he reached me, he whispered, "I'm sorry about this. I didn't know until the last minute you had been... sent for."

I chuckled, but leaned heavily against him. "It's okay," I whispered back. "But, for real, I'm so glad you came to get me. I'm one hundred percent sure I wouldn't have made it very far on my own."

"Nor should you," he said. "Come on."

He helped me into the front seat, next to his father. "It's a pleasure," I said to the man driving as I caught my breath.

He nodded at me, but didn't respond. *Okay*, I thought, *so it's going to be like that.*

No one spoke as we rode down the bumpy cobblestone road leading away from the clinic. Every bump hurt, so I held my hand over my chest and tried not to groan. Had I not been hurting; I would've paid more attention to how the carriage worked. Luckily, it didn't take long to get to their house, and, again with Conley's help, I returned to solid ground.

I was taken aback by the beautiful stone structure standing before us. It was mostly black granite, but there were streaks of red flowing through the stones, indicative of the fire-powered family that occupied it.

Conley helped me up the stairs to the front door, and as soon as we were inside, I was escorted to a front room. Conley's father continued ignoring me, but Conley helped me sit in a comfortable chair facing a fireplace with the fire banked inside.

"He doesn't seem happy I'm here," I said quietly to Conley, whose expression held concern. "Why *am* I here?"

He shrugged. "Like I said, I was only told moments before we left to get you that you were coming. I didn't even have time to dress."

It was as if his comment brought on a command. "Conley," a voice I recognized as his mother's called from somewhere toward the back of the home. "You need to change for dinner."

He sighed deeply, and said, "I'm so sorry." Then, he left me alone in the empty room.

I leaned back, the pain finally subsiding, and allowed myself to drift off. I still wasn't ready to be taking trips to meet the parents, but that was clearly not something they were concerned about. Gods, that didn't bode well for dinner.

I startled back to fully awake as I felt the weight of eyes on my body and opened mine to find Conley's parents staring at me. I sat up, feeling increasingly uncomfortable with the situation.

"Why are you here?" Mr. Bolcan asked, confusing me.

"Your wife told me to come," I said, sitting up and hoping that I hadn't just sounded like a smartass.

"No, in Dóiteán. Why are you here?"

His directness caught me off guard. I'd been asleep a moment before, and woke up to an inquisition. "I'm here because of my grandmother, but also because Conley said I was needed here. Why?" I asked, feeling defensive.

"You are an outsider. We have rules for how outsiders are to act when they come to Dóiteán, yet it seems you expect us to waive those rules for you."

That made me angry. Clearly, Conley's parents viewed me as the interloping boyfriend. I leaned up in my chair, ignoring the pain in my chest. "I have no expectations, and you have absolutely no right projecting your frustrations onto me. Why are you attacking me?" I asked.

By their shocked expressions, I could tell the couple wasn't used to being stood up to.

"You will not be disrespectful to us in our own home," Mrs. Bolcan said.

"Yet, you treat me with contempt after forcing me out of my sickbed and dragging me here. I am here to support your son, but if I'm not welcome in Dóiteán, I'll leave as soon as I am able," I said as I stood, and moved toward the front door.

I walked out of the room and caught sight of Conley on the stairs, his mouth hanging open. I shook my head. "I'm sorry, Conley, I'm clearly not welcome here. I'll try to find my way back to the clinic."

Ignoring the pain building by the second, I went out the front door. The moment the door closed behind me, a loud bang ripped through the village. The shockwave blew me back into the closed door.

People ran out of their homes and pointed up, and I saw one of the mountains had been the focus of the blast.

Huge balls of fire had been flung from the mountain and were falling into the forests around us. A round ring of red smoke circled the mountain—the red dragon. I knew the argument had caused the eruption, although my scientific mind certainly wanted to argue that a volcano couldn't possibly erupt just because it was mad. The flames now spreading through the forests suggested otherwise, though.

I managed to get myself down the stairs before collapsing onto a bench in the front garden. I heard the front door open behind me but didn't have the energy to turn around. A few moments later, Mr. Cho came rushing up the walkway. He looked at me, then at whoever stood in the doorway and shook his head. "You haven't learned anything from your parents' mistake, then," he said, then turned toward me. "Mr. Franklyn, come with me. We'll get you back to the clinic."

"Mr. Franklyn, wait," I heard Conley's father say.

I shook my head. "No, there's no waiting. I'm leaving."

"Of course, son, of course." I saw Mr. Cho give the other man a pointed look as he helped me to his carriage, not much different from the one I rode in to Conley's home. Back at the clinic, he tucked me in, did his mind-meld sleep spell on me again, and I was out.

The red dragon was livid. She stomped around the meadow, the one I'd met Conley in the first time.

"They have no right to send you away."

"They didn't," I said. The dragon's head spun toward me, and I could feel the fire on her breath. "They didn't send me away. I said I'd leave if I wasn't welcome."

"And they didn't stop you."

"Dearg, that's what they call you, right?" I asked, and the dragon's stare made me think she affirmed it. "They're parents. Parents are overprotective."

"They were rude to you."

I smiled. "Thank you for being concerned, but it's not worth erupting over. If you had a child, wouldn't you be as protective?" I asked. I had heard stories of dragons hoarding things since I was a child. I had no idea if that was true of these dragons or not, but I figured it would help her to see it from their perspective.

"Aye," she said, and I could feel some of her anger drain away. "We summoned you, because it is your destiny to be here, to help Conley find his way. Your father's curse has blended with the forces that have always pushed for chaos, always pushed for us to abandon our rational sensibilities. These things were predicted long, long ago, but it is your destiny to stop them with Conley's help."

I watched her, willing her to give me more information. My role in all this had always been vague, and I felt Conley was just as confused as I was.

When she didn't continue, I asked, "What would you have us do?"

"First, leave the village, they have forgotten their mission. You must bring Conley to me, and the two of you

must reside in the dwelling I've prepared for you. Let this be your time, and keep selfish parents from interfering."

I nodded, wanting to ask more questions, but I could tell it wasn't the time. I reached up, surprising myself, and placed my hand on the great dragon's face. "Calm. I won't leave Dóiteán, and when I'm recovered, I'll bring Conley to your cabin. You have no reason to be angry on my behalf, but I appreciate the sentiment."

She leaned against my hand momentarily, and then everything went black.

I woke up to the sound of Mr. Cho's voice. "It appears we only suppressed the barb's poison, because it wasn't fully healed. He's doing much better now. I suspect that was somehow Dearg's doing, although they seldom intervene. She was very... um... vocal yesterday."

I recognized Conley's voice then and moved to get up. "No, no, not yet," I heard someone say, and looked over to find a woman who looked a lot like Mrs. Bolcan, but older, and dressed in a traditional sari.

"I'm Mohini, Conley's grandmother," she said, and I cringed. "You have a right to react that way. But, unlike my daughter and son-in-law, I've learned my lesson when it comes to interfering with relationships."

I stared at her, not fully understanding and also more than a little bewildered at being woken to find Conley's family lurking around me.

She sighed when I didn't respond. "Do you remember when the mountain you call Mount St. Helens erupted?"

I shook my head. "Remember? No, that was before my time. I know of it though, I study volcanoes."

She chuckled sweetly. "Yes, I forget how young everyone is nowadays. Anyway, I was new to Dóiteán and still trying to find my footing when my daughter met and fell in love with one of the village's aristocracy."

"Let me guess, Mr. Bolcan?"

She nodded and continued to smile, but with a tinge of sadness. "His parents weren't happy that their son wanted to marry an outsider, I wasn't happy either, but that was for more selfish reasons. I didn't want to lose the one person I had who knew what we'd given up to come here."

"So, you tried to split them up?" I asked.

She nodded. "I did, and so did they. The kids ran away through the portal. At that time, the white dragon, the one we call Gael, was struggling with the pressure building up within her structure. That's the primary reason I'd been attracted to Dóiteán to begin with. I could feel her struggling and had been called here to settle her, to help calm her. The entire thing became so overwhelming, we forgot what we were doing, what we were here for, and as a result..."

"Mount St. Helens blew," I finished for her.

"Fifty-seven people lost their lives."

"You can't really believe it's your fault the mountain erupted," I said, ready to argue.

"No." She shook her head. "When a volcano is ready to go, it will go. Mother Nature, the Earth, they have their own agenda, but we were here to ease the pressure, to help minimize the loss."

"In a way, I guess you did, didn't you? I mean, it could've been so much worse."

"It wasn't me or the Bolcans who did that. The villagers gathered at the base of Gael and calmed her, brought her back into balance. After that," she said, sighing deeply, "...the village almost banished us, and rightfully so. With the help of Mr. Cho, we persuaded the village to give us another chance."

"Why are you telling me all this?" I asked.

"Because my daughter and son-in-law almost did the same thing last night."

"And," said Mr. Cho, who'd just stepped into the room, "...it could be even worse. If Conley's parents have driven a wedge between you, that could disrupt the dragons' plans. It could have devastating consequences."

I remembered Conley's shocked face when I left his house, and wasn't at all sure where things stood with us at the moment. I tried to get up, but I was still feeling really tired. "I'm sorry, but this is a bit much for me. I overdid it yesterday. I shouldn't have gone."

"No, you shouldn't have. Mrs. Bolcan went behind my back and against my recommendations in inviting you."

"That will not go over well with the council, especially since Dearg blew her top yesterday," Conley's grandmother confirmed. "I guess we should leave our guest to rest and go meet with the council. They will want your opinion."

Mr. Cho nodded. "Yes, they will, and yours too."

"That's unlikely," she said, and the way the two looked at one another, I knew there was more between them than friendship. I would've liked to have known more, but I just wanted to be left alone to rest.

I had just dozed off again when I heard a knock at my door. I looked up to see Conley standing awkwardly in the doorway.

"You okay?" I asked without moving to avoid causing myself undue pain.

"I should be asking you. I tried to visit last night, but Mr. Cho told me you needed rest. I'd have ignored him, except I could feel Dearg, and I didn't think I should do anything that might upset her more."

I chuckled quietly, trying not to stir too much. "She was pissed, that's for sure."

"Is she not pissed now?" he asked.

I smiled. "I think I've calmed her down, for now, but she won't be for long if we don't leave for the cabin she said she'd prepared for us."

He nodded. "It's a beautiful place, actually, with a fresh, clear stream running alongside it, and a forest with animals in abundance. It's much like you'd think heaven would be."

"You've been there then?" I asked, wanting to keep him engaged so he wouldn't leave.

"I've been there once in real life and several times in my dreams. It was built many years ago, and Dearg keeps it shrouded away, so it doesn't age."

"So, let's go."

"I'm afraid I have to deal with the fallout first, and that starts with you. I'm so sorry, Kyle. They had no right..."

"To love you? To be protective of you?" I asked. "You know my dad cursed me and my brothers because he's homophobic, right? He hasn't given a damn about us in years, if he ever did, which I'm beginning to wonder about. I'm not sure why your parents reacted like they did, but if it was to protect you, I'm not worried. The story your grandmother just told me indicates this is something they should've thought about more. I'm guessing that's something they're regretting at the moment anyway."

"They are, and they want to apologize. I told them to leave you alone."

I opened my arms, and Conley came over and crawled onto the bed next to me. "You don't hate me, do you?" he asked as my arms wrapped around him.

"No, can't say I'm extremely fond of your parents, but I do sorta like your grandma."

I could feel him smiling against me. "She's a character."

I could hear the humor in his voice and could only guess he was right. "So, when do we make the journey to the Red Dragon's Lair?" I asked, getting a snicker out of him.

"As soon as you feel up to it."

TWENTY-TWO

CONLEY

I COULDN'T BELIEVE MY parents. I mean, I knew they were strict. I knew they were overprotective, if not completely determined to keep anyone from ever showing any interest in me—at least, anyone they hadn't chosen themselves. But I'd never heard them be overtly rude.

I was shocked that Kyle had stood up to them. He'd done what I'd never had the nerve to do, not until now. "I can't believe you two. I can't believe you'd talk like that to someone, my guest. A guest of the dragons themselves."

If it hadn't been for the explosion and the fear I saw in their expressions, I was sure their response would've been belittling or condescending. As it was, they just stared at me, apparently stunned into silence.

"I'll be moving out," I said, and Mama gave a small whine, which almost made me feel bad about it. "I-I've never been so embarrassed in my life."

I could feel Dearg's feelings bombard me. She was so angry. I'd never experienced her like that before.

Honestly, it scared me. *"Dearg,"* I called out with my mind, but she didn't answer.

I rushed to the clinic, but Mr. Cho was there, as well as my grandmother. "You can't go in," Mr. Cho said, stopping me from pushing past them. "He's with Dearg. He's calming her."

I looked at him in shock. That was always my job. I forced down the spark of jealousy, knowing anyone able to calm the dragon, the volcano that loomed not far from our village, was smart to do so.

I plopped down in one of the uncomfortable waiting-room chairs, and after burying my face in my hands, I wept.

Grandma came over and put her arm around me. "He will sleep after he is done with the dragon. That's how it's always been, but when he wakes, he'll need you, want you."

"I don't know, Grandma, he was so upset."

"As are you, but you still care for him, do you not?"

I nodded, and she drew me into her arms. "Tonight, you will stay with Guha and me, and I will go speak with your parents. Then tomorrow, I will meet with your man. Conley, I'm not sure what got into your parents, but having been in the exact same place, I can only imagine how terrified they are. And sorry."

"I'm not worried about them. They treated Kyle poorly on purpose. But, yes, if you don't mind, I'd like to stay with you, at least until we can move to the cabin on Dearg's mountain. She's invited us there. It's part of why he's here."

She nodded, and for just a moment, I saw amusement in her eyes. Dearg's cabin had always been known as a place for lovers. We would be one couple of many to go live there, and for what? Lovemaking? I certainly hoped so, but also, I hoped it would be a place for us to be at peace. Even if the darkness loomed ever closer, we could hope Dearg's power would keep any interlopers at bay. And that included my parents.

I snuggled into Kyle's arms the next morning, so relieved he forgave me and didn't hold my parents' actions against me. Finally, after only tossing and turning the previous night, I fell asleep cuddled up against him.

I dreamed we were in the meadow again, lying in the old bed from the clinic. Kyle was asleep next to me.

I slipped off the bed, careful not to wake him, and looked up toward the sky. The darkness had grown and was pressing up against the three mountains. I could tell it wasn't able to penetrate them yet, which was some consolation, although I knew Dearg blowing yesterday had to do with the pressure the darkness was putting on them.

We needed to do something, and soon. Otherwise, things could get very ugly in both dimensions.

I heard rustling behind me and turned to see Gwen, Kyle's grandmother. I smiled at her. "You look rested. I'm happy about that."

"That's all down to my grandsons and you, of course."

"Me?" I asked, and she nodded. "You helped Kyle bring the fire. That weakened the darkness enough that I could banish it from me, but also separate it from my grandsons. You helped them burn away the curse they cast against their father."

"Then, what is that?" I asked, pointing toward the sky.

"That is more than just the curse," she said. "It's dark energy that's been fighting against the balance since the dawn of time. It feeds off negativity."

When I looked at her in confusion, she added, "Chaos is the ultimate creator. All things started out as chaos. But when it goes unchecked, it can be a destructive force. The energy you see here wishes to destroy."

"So, it's evil?"

She shook her head. "No, chaos isn't evil, it's just chaos. For it to create, it must destroy. These dragons, as you call them, were designed by the Earth to create more Earth. And before humans came to live here, they did so unchecked. Only in the past few thousand years has a balance been created. When the first humans came to this land, the volcanoes became sentient. Now they are in a constant battle between the desire to create and the desire to protect what they currently nourish."

"So, what? That darkness is somehow forcing the issue?" I asked.

"Yes and no. It's only dark because of the curse my son cast upon his children. Otherwise, the energy would still be clear, always present, but never malevolent. Not like it is now."

"We need to go to Dearg soon, don't we?" I asked, already knowing the answer.

"Yes, young one, that's why I've come. I must help you cross the boundary, help you and my grandson restore balance and shift the current away from that," she said, pointing up at the sky.

"How are we to do that? Kyle is injured," I said and could almost hear the defeat in my voice.

"Oh, well," she said, smiling, "this is where having a spirit passing between the dimensions helps. She walked over to where Kyle still lay sleeping, lifted her hands, and began chanting...

"Ether gray and darkness thrust,
Know thy hatred is unjust,
I call upon the spirits here,
To bring out the darkness that fights with fear..."

Gwen reached over Kyle's still sleeping form and made a pulling motion. A cloudlike mist rose up from Kyle's chest. I could feel the same tug in my own, and when I reached up and touched my chest, she smiled.

"Yes, that should take care of you both."

"What? Wait? You mean..."

"Yes, child, that's why my son's cantation was dogging me so hard. You being here, on this side of the dimension, allows me to heal you both. Now, let's wake my grandson."

I felt where my heart still stung slightly and couldn't help but be amazed at how quickly she was able to repair the damage. Five years at most, that's what the Fire Guild couple had told me I had left in this life. In less time, I'd begin to lose function in my heart. Mr. Cho had confirmed it, promising me once Kyle was out of danger, he'd help us both, but...

"Just like that?" I asked aloud, and the woman laughed.

"No, it was a great deal more than just like that, but because of the dragons and what you and my grandsons did the night they strengthened me, it was possible to do this for you now."

She turned to Kyle. "Kyle, honey, it's time to wake up."

Kyle stretched and yawned. "Grandma? Is it time already?"

"Yes, grandson, you must get up."

His eyes opened in surprise. "I dreamed I was in high school. Grandma, you were waking me up."

"That was for me," she said. "Just wanted a moment to remember. But time has run out, and you must go to the cabin on Dearg's mountain. You must help her and the others keep the darkness at bay. Come now."

She began walking away, and I reached over to offer Kyle my hand so we could follow. He got up and moved like he was completely without pain.

"Wow, I feel great," he said as he took my hand.

"That's your grandmother's doing," I began before being interrupted.

"Are you boys coming?" Gwen yelled, and Kyle laughed.

"Death hasn't changed her one bit."

"I can hear you, Kyle," she scolded.

"You raised me to speak the truth," he said, and with his hand in mine, he pulled me toward where his grandmother had gone. It felt good to run with him again. Carefree and without the distractions of either of our families, well, aside from his spirited grandmother.

Twenty-Three

Kyle

GRANDMA WALKED AHEAD OF us the entire time. No matter how fast we ran or what terrain we crossed, we remained behind her. "Grandma, why are you in such a hurry?"

She looked up at the sky, and when my eyes followed, I could see we were now underneath the darkness. She didn't respond, but moved her hand to indicate we should hurry.

I started coughing immediately. It became almost impossible to breathe, like something was pressing against my chest.

The dark became more and more oppressive the further we hiked, and at one point it felt as if we were slogging through mud. The darkness surrounded us now, and it smelled of ash and burnt plastic.

Clumps of burnt debris, like burning leaves, swirled around us. I was surprised we weren't suffocating, not that my breathing had improved any. The darkness in some areas seemed to take form, like some threatening, monstrous creatures that loomed around us, which significantly upped the feeling of doom.

I knew it was just an illusion, but that didn't ease my mind much. A feeling I was becoming way too familiar with I once again felt, as if we were going to die here.

Just when I thought we wouldn't be able to move any further, we came to its border. Just like that, we had crossed out of the darkness and were back in the light.

Grandma paused to let us catch our breath. "You waited so long. We were lucky to get through as easily as we did."

When I looked at her, though, I realized it hadn't been quite so easy on her. Where her body had looked solid in the meadow, it was nearly transparent now, and I could tell she was barely maintaining herself in this realm.

"Are you okay?" I asked.

She waved me off. "Yes, I'm fine, but I'll have to be away for a while. Don't let that worry you, though, the dragons will take it from here."

I looked up to see all three dragons flying overhead. Grandma looked up and smiled, then she kissed me and waved at Conley before she disappeared.

After that, we walked through the trees into a clearing, at which point, the dragons glided down toward us. The moment they touched down, all three changed shape and took on human forms.

"Whoa," both Conley and I said at the same time.

"Um, you're human now?" Conley asked.

"Welcome to our domain," Dearg said, and winked at Conley, not answering his question. "Now, let us show you to your cabin."

Twenty-Four

Conley

I WATCHED IN UTTER amazement as the dragons flew down from the sky. As light began to sparkle around them, they slowly transformed from the huge reptilian creatures I'd known them to be all my life to... humans. Like, actual flesh and blood people.

To be honest, I wasn't sure if I actually believed what I was seeing. Only their hair color–black, red, and white–hinted at their former dragon forms. Could we still call them dragons?

None of us spoke as Kyle and I followed them. Eventually, we reached the cabin, and I remembered coming here multiple times before. Except this time, it was different. Newer almost.

The furniture gleamed like it had never been used. Appliances, similar to those found in the village, sat in pristine condition along the kitchen wall. When I couldn't resist and pulled the refrigerator door open, it was full of food.

"H-how?" I asked.

The red-haired woman–Dearg, I reminded my-self–smiled. "You are in our territory now. It is there because we willed it."

"Are you gods?" Kyle asked, and all three chuckled.

"We are what we are," the white-haired woman–Gael–answered.

"And you must be Dubh," I said, turning to the man who'd retained his larger size along with his black hair color. He grinned and nodded at me... he was clearly a man of few words, too.

"But why are you human... or, well, whatever you are now?" Kyle asked.

"Because, this is how we see ourselves these days. We are a representation of the human lives around us. We are also the wildlife that lives on our mountainsides. Would you feel more comfortable if we took their form?" Gael asked.

"No, this will just take a little getting used to is all."

Dearg laughed. "Well, we wouldn't fit into the cabin as dragons anyway. Besides, that is your ancestors' view of us. We simply became dragons to accommodate them."

"Will you stay with us?" Kyle asked, which earned another laugh from Dearg. "Certainly not," she said. "As much as I like to matchmake, I do not wish to watch. We only wanted to welcome you here. You will be on your own when we leave, and you will have complete privacy."

"We've waited a very long time for you to join us, Conley, and you too, Kyle," Gael added, "...although we didn't really know about you until recently."

Kyle smiled and nodded. "Thank you, and the plea-sure is mine."

The three figures bowed and left. I was still mesmerized by their transformation.

"Let's explore," Kyle said, taking my hand and leading me upstairs. There was a huge bedroom with a balcony that looked out over a beautiful landscape. The cabin had been built high on a ridge that must've been an old lava flow, because no trees grew in front of us, giving us a breathtaking view.

When I'd been here before, the windows had been too dirty to see out of, but not now. Now you could see for miles through the crystal-clear panes.

I turned back toward the bed and was pleased to find clean bedding. Had I come up alone, I'd have packed my own set. Well... or bought a new set, considering I wasn't willing to go back to my parents to ask for anything.

"Do you think we're still dreaming?" Kyle asked as he opened the closet, and found both his and my clothes hanging up and neatly stacked on the shelves.

"Does it feel like a dream?" I asked.

"No, but it seems hard to accept that one minute I'm lying in a clinic and the next I'm here in this incredible cabin with three volcano people as our hosts."

"It's Dóiteán, stranger things have happened."

Kyle came over and pulled me into a hug that ended with him lying on top of me on the bed. "Is that so?" he asked, teasing. "And what is stranger than this, Conley Bolcan?"

"Oh, you know, watching your grandmother's spirit remove dark energy from your heart before curing us both. That was pretty extraordinary."

"Wow, she did that?" he asked.

"Yep, and said we were both cured."

"You too? Like, no dying in five years?" he asked, and I could see the concern in his eyes.

I shook my head. "Apparently not."

I squirmed to get comfortable under Kyle, and when I did, his expression grew heated. "Wanna get naked with me?" he asked, nuzzling my neck.

Yes! I thought, but maybe not with three dragon people hanging around. To be honest, the three of them felt more like parents than anything else, so I shrugged. "I think I need some time to know they aren't still lurking around."

Kyle laughed and rolled off me. "We can make out, though, right?"

"Oh yeah," I agreed, and pressed my lips to his.

Twenty-Five

Kyle

It was strange that a dream brought us from Dóiteán to living in a cabin. It felt different from our other shared dreams though. This felt more real.

Also real was how much I wanted Conley, more than ever, and I was determined to have him, even if it meant we had to wait until he was comfortable.

When I walked downstairs the next morning, after falling asleep with him in my arms, I could smell something cooking in the kitchen. "Wow, you're making breakfast?" I asked.

"Yep," he said as he poured me a cup of coffee. "I think I made it how you like it."

I tasted it and smiled. "Perfect," I replied, reaching over the counter to kiss him. "What's on the agenda for today?" I asked.

"Not sure, but I'm guessing not much since we're in the middle of nowhere and no one has told us we have any tasks to do. I thought maybe a hike through the trail system that loops through these parts."

"I love hiking. I used to be more active before I started grad school, but not so much lately. But I didn't bring hiking boots."

"Didn't you?" he asked, and pointed toward the door. Two brand new pairs were sitting next to one another.

"You sure this isn't still a dream?"

He shrugged, and said, "Does it matter? Whether we're in your dimension, mine, or our shared dream state in the meadow, we're together. Isn't that enough for now?"

"Yes," I said without having to think about it.

After breakfast, we put on the boots that fit like they were well-worn, as well as clothes that looked perfect for the climate, and took off away from the cabin.

Deer bounded in front of us, seemingly unafraid. At one point, we saw a mountain lion lying lazily in a tree, and decided to go a different direction to avoid it. We saw a bear a few miles later and did the same. A little further, and the trail wound past a herd of huge elk in an open meadow.

I looked out over the forest, and realized this was what it must've felt like before European settlers in my dimension began cutting down the old-growth forests and killing all the wildlife. It was truly a paradise. For the umpteenth time, I had to wonder what would cause the early settlers to deliberately destroy a place like this.

We hiked for what felt like hours until we were both beginning to feel hungry. Unfortunately, we were so eager to hit the trail that we completely forgot to pack lunch. Maybe that was something we should remember for the next hike.

Conley took his backpack off, rummaged through it, and smiled when he found a granola bar from my side of the portal. "Um, well, apparently, we're being taking care of now."

I looked around the forest to see if anyone was watching us. No, it truly felt like we were alone.

"Okay, well, let's not question it. I'll split that with you."

The rest of the day was exactly the same, beautiful scenery with wild animals at every turn. None of them seemed the least bit concerned about our existence, which was lucky, because some of them weren't small.

By the time we got back to the cabin, we were both physically tired, but happy. We pulled our boots off, hung up our jackets, and walked into the kitchen to begin preparing dinner. But, to our surprise, a ready meal sat on the counter along with a note.

Don't worry about cooking, we did it for you, just enjoy. Oh, and there are hot springs out the back about a quarter-mile into the woods.

It was signed *Red*.

"They are trying," I said and couldn't help but smile at the overt efforts of, at the very least, Dearg's matchmaking.

"Maybe a bit too much. Can you make a concealment spell?" Conley asked.

"Um, maybe. I did something similar when I was a kid with my grandma's coven, but it's usually done with air. It's not a strong spell with fire energy."

"What if we had liquid fire flowing under us?"

"It's worth a try, but liquid fire and cabins don't go together. Let's try it in a clearing or maybe at those hot springs," I said, and wiggled my eyebrows.

"Okay, let's eat first, then the hot springs."

I stripped the moment we reached the springs, not even thinking about Conley being more timid. I'd grown up with brothers, participated in athletic sports in high school, and as a gay man... well, it never seemed to be a problem.

I climbed into the hot water and groaned. My hiking-tired muscles seemed to sigh with happiness as the heat engulfed them.

I looked back to find Conley staring at me, frozen. "Um, Conley, are you okay?" I asked.

He shook his head. "I'm... I think I'm going to go back to the cabin."

"Oh no, wait," I said, and began to crawl out of the water.

"No, no I... I'm..."

I reached him and found him shaking. "Honey, what's wrong? What's happening?"

"I'm no good at this. I suck at it. I'm so afraid you won't find me attractive. I'm fat and have a smart mouth."

"Not a chance. First of all, I adore your mouth, especially when it's kissing mine," I said, which earned me a small smile. "Second, you aren't fat. I've already told you how much I like your body. Do you have underwear on?" I asked and he nodded.

"Okay, leave them on if it makes you feel better. We're not in a rush here, Conley. I just want to enjoy all of this with you. If we aren't... if we don't ever do anything other than what we have already done, that's okay. Okay?" I asked and he nodded again. "In that case, slip your clothes off and join me. The water is perfect."

I purposely walked away with my back turned and got back into the pool, lying back with my eyes closed. A few moments later, I heard him hiss as his body slipped into the warm water.

When I opened my eyes, he was looking at me, those big brown eyes roaming over my face. "What?" I asked, concerned.

"Why are you so patient with me? Do you no longer want me?"

I couldn't help but laugh. "Conley, I've never wanted anyone like I want you. Every time I look at you, there's something new that I didn't notice before, something that makes me want you even more. But I've been a virgin, I know how difficult it is to trust someone enough to give yourself to them. To let them in enough to enjoy your body and for you to enjoy theirs."

"So, you're just taking things slow for my sake?"

I smiled because it was true, I really was just being patient. "I am here for when you're ready, but not one minute before. For now, come over here and sit next to me. This is pure heaven."

He smiled and floated over to me. "You know I really do like you. I want... all of it. You know that, right?"

"I do," I said confidently.

"And, if I wasn't so awkward..."

"Shh," I chastised. "Enough of that. You're perfect how you are."

I laid my head back against one of the smooth rocks lining the pool and let the heat pull all the tension from my body. I felt Conley shift, and when I looked up, he was in front of me. "Can I try something?" he asked, sounding a bit shy.

I nodded silently as he moved closer. His hand slid up my chest as he crept into my arms. Then I felt his cock rub against mine and my eyes widened at the realization he hadn't kept his underwear on.

He moaned softly as he glided against me, our cocks both hardening as they touched.

"You sure?" I asked, and he nodded, his expression filled with desire.

He clung to my shoulders as his legs wrapped around my waist, his ass brushing over my cock, shocking me. He wasn't exactly acting like someone who hadn't had sex before.

I couldn't help but thrust against him, although I did so gently, so as not to scare him away.

"I-I watched how to do this on your computers. I-I'm still not sure what to do exactly, but it feels so good," he said, and I couldn't help but smile.

"This is a lot for a beginner. You think you'd like to take me inside you?" He blushed and nodded. "Okay, but that takes prep. Do you trust me?" I asked.

He nodded again and I kissed him, then grabbed hold of his thighs and hoisted us both out of the water. I directed him get on all fours and began to move my finger around his hole, slowly massaging the opening until I could tell he was enjoying the sensation.

Using my own spit, I began to glide a finger inside him, and he immediately relaxed, moaning.

"I'm going to use my tongue now," I whispered.

I figured he'd freak out about that. I knew the first time I'd considered eating ass, it had freaked me out, but when he nodded enthusiastically, I assumed it was something he'd seen on the internet.

I leaned in and began to run my tongue over the sensitive tissue around his hole. When he bucked up against my mouth, I knew he was okay, so I thrust my tongue all the way inside.

"Gods!" he cried out. Knowing I was giving him pleasure like this for the first time made my heart skip a beat.

Then I slipped my finger into his hole. "Push down on my finger," I instructed. "If it hurts, let me know."

He nodded as I slowly massaged my finger in and out, letting him relax before trying to insert another.

"Gods, you're so hot," I said when he began to fuck himself on my fingers. Three, how the hell could he be taking all three of my fingers already?

I stood up and pulled him back into the pool, wanting him to feel me... *us*... before we went all the way.

When we were both back in the warm water, I began kissing him while jacking him off. "You're so beautiful, Conley. I want you so bad."

His eyes glazed over with lust and our tongues tangled as I continued stroking him and let my finger resume massaging his hole.

When I could tell he was fully relaxed, I guided him to lie on the flat rock at the side of the pool with his ass on the edge. I lifted his legs, so they rested on my shoulders, and took his cock into my mouth.

"Mmm, oh my gods," he moaned as I began to suck him. Shock waves pulsed through me as I showed Conley everything sex could be. I wanted this to be special. I needed him to know the pleasure one could feel from making love with another man.

I'd had a complete physical after returning to campus from Mexico and knew I was disease-free. And him being a virgin, there was no chance of him giving me anything, so I wasn't worried about needing protection.

Still, it was a big step for us, and I had to make sure he understood.

"Are you sure? We don't have any condoms, obviously," I said, running my hands up and down his thighs.

He gazed at me hungrily and nodded. "I trust you, Kyle," he said, and leaned forward to kiss me. When our lips parted, I went about prepping him again, lubing his ass with spit until he was fully pliable.

Satisfied he was ready to take me, I climbed out of the water, and we shifted to a grassy area next to the spring. Then I lubed my own cock and lined myself up to his hole. I slowly pushed inside, and he drew in a deep breath. "Relax, baby, now try to push against me."

He nodded again and began to move, his body naturally seeking pleasure. I let him control most of the movement, only stopping occasionally to moisten myself or to keep his cock lubed for maximum pleasure as I jacked him off.

Finally, he pushed against me, taking my cock all the way inside him. "Fuck," he said, and tensed.

I pulled out and leaned over to kiss him. "Don't be in too much of a hurry. Just go slow, and move only when you feel comfortable."

He nodded, and I probed him with my fingers again.

This time when I lined my cock up, he immediately took control and slowly began to fuck me from below. I moved back and forth, encouraging him to feel the pleasure beside the pain, and within moments he began to moan as he took my cock deeper and deeper.

Never before had I felt something so magical, so amazing. Conley was tight, impossibly so, and I was ready to stop at any moment, but he clearly wanted this.

His long moans only spurred me on, and it was all I could do not to thrust hard into him. When he had worked me fully inside, we stayed like that for several seconds before he looked up at me and smiled.

Oh, my heart, that smile did so many strange things to it. I leaned down, still inside him, and ravaged his adorable mouth.

"Now, let me pleasure you," I said against his wet lips.

When he nodded eagerly, I began to thrust, gently at first, as he got used to the sensation of being fucked for the first time.

Then, as he got used to me, I picked up the pace and began thrusting harder and deeper into him. His body responded with each snap of my hips, taking everything I was giving.

I began to lose myself in the pleasure of fucking Conley. He looked completely blissed out, and his moans pushed me to give him even more.

I was jacking him off in rhythm to my thrusts when he pressed down on my cock, cried out, and came all over his chest. His eyes registered surprise from the intensity of the orgasm as they locked onto mine.

I pulled out before my own orgasm hit, then jacked myself off as I came all over his chest and cock.

"Gods, Conley," I yelled as the orgasm swept through me, "...you're so fucking hot!"

When I was spent, I collapsed, half on the grass, half lying on his warm body.

When I was finally able to get my brain to engage again, I leaned up on my elbow, looking down at him. Seeing his sleepy, sexually satisfied eyes and lazy grin caused my heart to race again. "You okay?" I asked, stroking his jawline with my thumb.

"Mmmm," he moaned. "That was amazing."

I chuckled. "You're going to be sore. Come back in the water with me."

We climbed onto the naturally smooth rock that lined the pool. As he curled into me, we drifted to sleep with him in my arms. It'd been a good first experience for him, and out of this world for me. All of a sudden, I totally understood what it meant to lose your heart to someone.

✧

We woke the next morning in our bed, my arms still wrapped around him. When Conley looked at me in confusion, I shook my head. "Okay, for real, we're in the dream state. I know we fell asleep at the hot springs." He nodded and stretched. "Are you okay?" I asked, hoping the happy smile on his face indicated he was.

He closed the distance and kissed me. "I'm great. More than great. But damn, I want coffee."

"Agreed, I'm so glad you have coffee here. Do you have runners who go out to collect it?"

He shook his head. "No, I didn't get to show you around Dóiteán. There are farms stretched across the region that grow things that wouldn't normally grow in your area across the portal. Like coffee, chocolate, citrus."

He climbed out of bed and my eyes raked over his naked body before he slipped on a robe that was hanging on a peg next to the closet. "It helps to be a fire-based community since generating heat is easy, especially when it lurks just meters under your feet."

"That's good and bad," I said, thinking of all the ways lava flowing close to the surface could create damage.

He must've noticed my concern and smiled. "You have to remember, we're mostly fire-based energy here. If something is about to go off, we usually know it."

"Like the explosion from your parents?"

He cringed. "No, clearly the pressures can get away from us. And there's no one who fully understands the dragons... should I still call them that? Well, whatever they are, no one knows when their emotions will shift or change."

"It's still so strange to me. How do you control the volcanic flow and stop the eruptions?"

"Let's go have breakfast. I'll answer your questions as best as I can. Anything I can't answer, Mr. Cho or my... well, Mr. Cho can."

"You were going to say your dad," I said, feeling sad about how things turned out.

"Yeah, that didn't end well. I never expected them to lash out at anyone, let alone someone I brought home. Usually, my parents' irrational frustrations and inappropriate outbursts are reserved for me."

"Did they abuse you? Hurt you?"

He shook his head. "No, nothing like that. More like they love me *too* much. They can barely let me go or let me do anything. Unfortunately, all these years, I've let them. I have so few real-life experiences... well, until now." He looked at me with a sly grin. "I'm hoping to do that again and soon, please."

"After breakfast?" I asked, climbing out of bed, and pulling him into my embrace. He hummed in agreement before I let him go, then I slipped on my own robe as we headed downstairs.

We spent the morning with him filling me in on all the wonders of Dóiteán. The people here used their skills in the most amazing ways. I had never thought of using fire energy to heat greenhouses, or in this case, entire fields.

I really wanted to see it all, to spend time here to learn all their secrets. Of course, what would that mean for my life back home? I had literally just turned in my dissertation for my Ph.D.

I wouldn't know my dissertation committee's decision for at least another few weeks, but I was confident that I'd finally completed my education. Would I be willing to trade years and years of work to live in a place like Dóiteán?

Not that Conley had proposed, or that I bought into the fairytale of eternal love. We'd had sex. Mind-blowing, soul-reaching sex, but it was just sex. Of course, I knew that wasn't quite right either. There was no denying I was developing real feelings for Conley, but I didn't want to mess things up by being overly focused on what came next in our relationship.

Maybe that was how I should be treating my place here in Dóiteán. Conley had described how the people here were responsible for creating vents in the three dragon mountains, keeping steam and gasses from building up too much pressure. The Earth was quieted as well. That took the most time and effort for the community.

In my dimension, the eruption of Mount St. Helens—or Gael, as they called her here—was caused when a five-point-one earthquake caused a landslide that shifted the pressure where the magma chamber lay. That caused the side of the mountain to explode. At the time, the Dóiteán villagers knew there was an eruption looming and were trying to correct it. As Conley's grandmother told me, their family drama had distracted the community just enough that the earthquake got away from them before they could calm it.

Even in my studies, there'd been discussions—all theoretical, of course, since we couldn't control the earth—about creating fissures so pressure could be released. We might not have been able to prevent the Mount St. Helens landslide, but if the pressure had been reduced, the subsequent explosion could've been less impactful.

Of course, we'd never discussed the power of a community of fire elementals living in a parallel dimension to shift that balance. I chuckled to myself, thinking how Dr. Fagan—the respected, highly analytical, no-nonsense professor—would've handled that as a safer solution for volcanism around populated areas.

"You could be a professor," I told Conley.

"Why do you say that?" he asked, confusion evident in his expression.

"You explain things so well, so intricately, but you aren't boring about it. Do you have universities or colleges here?"

He smiled. "Yes, I went to college, as you call it. I graduated with high marks, but I'm not really teacher material."

"Trust me, I've been in school most of my life. I even taught classes at the university. You have the skills."

He blushed a little, then went quiet. Clearly, he wasn't used to receiving compliments.

"I don't know what the future holds for me, since I'm not like my father. I have no interest in becoming the leader of Dóiteán. I've told him repeatedly they should start holding elections like they do on your side of the portal, but he's never been willing to accept that. Our family has ruled Dóiteán for over a century and a half. But it's grown so much. It really shouldn't be under one family's leadership any longer." He shook his head. "I'm sorry to bring all my family drama up. Anyway, tell me more about... you know..."

He smiled at me then, and I knew he was referring to my dad's ever-present curse.

I took a deep breath and let it out slowly. "I've never told anyone about it. Well, except for my friend Yvonne. Never a guy... boyfriend. Are we boyfriends?" I asked, mostly to stall.

His smile brightened. "Yeah, I like that description."

I sighed inwardly, relieved we were on the same page about our relationship, then launched into it. "I was just a kid, not even a teenager," I said, and walked toward the living room, crashing heavily down on the sofa as Conley settled in next to me. "I'd been having feelings for this guy on my baseball team. He was taller than me, had strong features and skin the color of ebony. He was so handsome. I remember obsessing about how smooth his skin looked. Anyway, I mustered up the courage to tell my brothers, who were both already sorta out of the closet, but we'd never talked about it."

"So? What happened next?" he asked, and I groaned, knowing it was important to get all this out, but damn, I didn't like rehashing it.

"So, I told my brothers I wanted to tell Mom and Dad. It seemed so important at the time. To this day, I don't know why it mattered so much."

"It mattered because they were your family, and you wanted them to understand you."

I reached over and took Conley's hand, feeling his sadness regarding his own parents and their lack of support for his love life.

"My brothers thought it would be no big deal. I mean, Chemeketa, where Dad had grown up, was intensely supportive regardless—gay, lesbian, transgender, all the other alphabet soup..." I paused when he looked confused. "On my side of the dimension, we use the acronym LGBTQ+ as an umbrella term to describe sexual orientations and gender identities. It came about as a way to promote a unified cause for equality. It stands for Lesbian, Gay, Bisexual, Transgender, Queer or Questioning, and the plus includes people who only desire sexual relations with people they have feelings for, people who are not sexual at all... it's all very inclusive," I said, trying to stay out of the weeds too much. "Anyway, we call that LGBTQ+, hence the alphabet soup comment."

He nodded in understanding, so I pressed on with my sad story.

"Well, so we didn't think coming out would be an issue, or at least, Lance and Crea didn't. Our great-grandfather, dad's grandfather, was a bisexual man. He had a male lover and a wife at the same time. They all lived together in the house Drew lives in now. So then, why would Dad care if his sons weren't straight, right?"

I drew in another deep breath and rubbed the back of my neck as I admitted the truth I'd never told anyone else. "I think deep down, I knew he'd have an issue with it. Lance and Crea were born when Dad and Mom were much more laid back. They'd spent much more time in Chemeketa during those early years, but when I was around five, my grandfather Franklyn died. Something shifted in my dad after that. I don't think Lance and Crea really saw it, not the way I did. He became much less... available? I don't know. My five-year-old self didn't really have the words for it, and I still don't, but his spirit changed after his father's death. We visited Chemeketa less and less, and eventually he stopped taking us to see Grandma altogether."

Conley didn't say anything, just squeezed my hand in understanding, which I took as my cue to continue.

"My mom's parents are wealthy, like, crazy rich. They own grocery stores all over the western half of the country. After Grandpa Franklyn died, they began pulling Dad and Mom into their world, and even convinced Dad to convert to Catholicism. The three of us refused to do so, and even Grandma Gwen stepped in to say that had to be our choice, not theirs. That, of course, only made my mom hate her, and didn't stop Mom from sending me to a Catholic school and trying to involve me in the church. I won't go into details, just suffice it to say, the family was splintering, and I was aware of it even at that age."

I stared out at the beautiful view, seeing but not really seeing it. Memories of that awful night swirled in my mind, the feelings of guilt and devastation as fresh as when it happened. "I didn't even know Lance was going to come out to them. He just said they wouldn't care, and I think he truly believed it. But that night, as we sat at the dinner table, off the cuff, he just said, 'You all know I'm gay, right?' My mom gasped, and my dad's face contorted into this angry scowl. But it wasn't about us at all, not really. My parents' reactions were all about their own desires for my father to hold political office. Long story short, my dad cursed us that night, using magic he'd supposedly forsaken for his new religion. I honestly can't remember the exact words of the curse. I was crying too hard by then. It was something along the lines of us boys never finding love with another man. He condemned us to be alone forever... and..."

I was beginning to choke up when Conley raised my hand to his lips and gently kissed my knuckles. He was such a caring man. "I saw the darkness flow into my father as he cursed us. I saw that," I said, pointing up at the dark that lurked just outside the dragons' circle of protection. "He was letting it flow in, letting himself embrace the darkness. To this day, I still don't understand why."

I felt the tears slide down my face, and I didn't resist when Conley put his arms around me, pulling me into his embrace.

I cried for a while, letting out the years of pent-up emotions I'd kept locked inside. I'd been so afraid I'd lose myself and everything I loved if I didn't hold on tight to my sadness.

But Conley was the antidote to that poison. Having him so near convinced me I could let it go without fear as the cold glacier around my heart melted.

After a long cry, I wiped away the tears and gave a wet chuckle. "Then, Lance cursed Dad right back, and told him that he'd lose us forever. I felt energy coming from Crea and myself as we allowed it to happen. Really, we *made* it happen. That's the curse we broke the other day when we were all standing around the fire, and Grandma Gwen came."

Conley nodded, acknowledging he'd figured that much out on his own.

"Anyway, and this is probably the ugliest part of all this, I didn't mind my dad's curse. To be honest, I embraced it. Whenever a guy started to get close to me, I'd imagine my dad's face that night. The face that had once been one of love and commitment to his family and had morphed into pure hatred and vengeance. In my heart, I accepted that any man I loved would eventually become like him. So, I kept them all out. Unlike Lance and Crea, who had horrible relationship after horrible relationship fall apart around them, I never put myself out there on purpose. If you don't let them in, they can't hurt you."

"You let me in though," Conley said quietly, speaking for the first time.

"I did, and I'll continue to. The night we stood around the fire, Grandma helped me realize I needed to remove my walls. She helped me see that I had to let go of the past, if I ever wanted to find happiness. And I am happy, being here with you."

I leaned back into Conley and sighed as we reclined together on the sofa. "That doesn't mean this is easy for me. Sometimes the thought of a long-term relationship makes me want to run screaming into the night. I've ghosted men before, which means disappearing without a trace, but I'm afraid even pretending to be a ghost might give my real ghost grandmother the power to kick my butt. That scares me more than a relationship does."

Conley chuckled, and I could feel the vibration in his chest. "Trust me, I know all about interfering grand-mothers."

I snuggled back into him, smiling. "I think your grand-ma is sweet."

"She is, and she's almost as overprotective as my par-ents are. Although, I don't think she has the same need to control my every movement."

"We come from such different backgrounds," I said. "My dad and mom threw us away, and yours can't let go."

Conley wrapped his arms tighter around me. "Your grandmother, Gwen, seems to adore you guys."

I smiled at that. "She was the most amazing woman. I loved her with everything I had in me, still do. In truth, she saved us. Even in death, she's doing everything she can to save us. Without her, I think we'd all be lost."

We lay back like that, quietly letting the conversation linger between us. Finally, Conley said, "I don't want you to feel like I'm smothering you. I needed you... needed what we did last night. The world clicked into place, and something that had been missing seemed to repair itself inside me. But, that doesn't mean you are obligated..."

"I don't feel obligated. I feel as though what we have is something special. I want it, and I want you. Don't overthink it, okay?" I asked, and could hear the pleading in my voice.

I glanced up to see him smiling at me, and he nodded. "Okay, but if you ever feel smothered, just tell me, okay? Whatever I'm doing that makes you feel uncomfortable, I-I can always back off."

"Liar," I said, chuckling. "Baby, I've only known you a short time, but I can tell you go all in." I kissed him as I tried to make things lighter. "And that's exactly what I need right now, especially while I'm scared to death you'll turn into my father. I need you to be all you are, okay?"

He smiled and pushed me down onto the sofa, rolling on top of me. "I'm going to be all in *now*," he said, and kissed me deeply.

Twenty-Six

Conley

Listening to Kyle tell his story was heartbreaking. My parents were a lot, but they'd never gone so far as to curse me. It took hatred to curse someone—deep-seated hatred. That was something we learned early on in our education.

Anything that tipped the balance, hatred included, was something that had to be managed this close to the dragons. So, Mr. Cho had spent weeks every year as we progressed through school emphasizing how important balance was to the wellbeing of our community and to our collective mission.

I wonder if Kyle really understood what his father's curse had entailed. As I listened to him explain, I had to assume at least a part of him did. My heart hurt for him and his brothers. It hurt so much more, though, for the boy who'd watched his father betray him that day.

That afternoon, we hiked—mostly in silence—through the forests that led over to Dubh's mountain. Something in me knew Kyle needed time to process that morning's discussion. There was a river that separated Dubh from Dearg. Usually, it wasn't very deep, mostly made up of the glacial melt from atop Dubh. As we drew closer, I heard the gushing of the water, which surprised me. This time of year, the river should've been nothing more than a trickle as the glacier would be almost completely frozen.

Then, I saw what I'd heard. Water flowed, dark and foreboding, between the river's banks, threatening to spill over. I immediately reached out to Dubh in my mind.

"Great dragon, why are your glaciers melting so fast?"

When he appeared to us, he was back in his dragon form. That prevented him from speaking, but I could hear him loud and clear in my mind, and I knew Kyle could as well.

"This is the warning we've been giving you. The darkness that lurks outside our boundaries is building against us. As a result, our fires build within us. The ice that sits atop my mountain is melting from the heat."

"Are you afraid of erupting?" Kyle asked aloud, concern lacing his voice.

"My fire has been asleep for thousands of years. Thanks to the people of Dóiteán, the pressure within my core is minimal. But yes, if it continues to push against us, eventually even my fires, sleepy as they are, will burst forth."

"What about Gael, Dearg?" I asked.

Dubh lowered his head. I heard the wings of the other dragons before I saw them as they landed next to him. *"My fires aren't asleep, but they are calm,"* Gael said, answering my question. *"My mountain will simply rebuild for many, many years to come."*

"But," Dearg added, *"as you've already seen, my fire is restless. It hungers to break forth."*

"Where are you in my world, Dearg?" Kyle asked.

At that, she split into three smaller dragons. All red. One was old, another young, and the third middle-aged, looking more like the Dearg we all knew.

"Three Sisters," he said.

"Don't make any assumptions, young Kyle," Dubh said. *"We may have physical manifestations in your world, but we represent all the volcanic activity in this part of what you call the Ring of Fire. In some ways, we represent all volcanic activity on what you also call the North and South American continents."*

I shook my head in confusion. *"The people of Dóiteán came to this region because we are the most active volcanoes on this continent,"* Dearg said, resuming her form as one dragon. *"We represent who Conley's ancestor saw as she came to this area. The ones she knew were the greatest threat. So, when she summoned us, she only brought forth the three of us."*

"So, what, there are more of you, more I've never met?" I asked, surprised at this new perspective. It turned everything my community thought we knew about the dragons on its head.

"Not in our form, no. Your ancestor, Luna Raven, embedded herself in our form. We are in part a manifestation of her, but we are connected to all our siblings, especially here in this part of the continent."

"So, you know of the impending threat no matter where it's occurring."

All three dragons lowered their heads in acknowledgment. "In a way, that's reassuring. In another, I'm more concerned now than ever," Kyle said. "So, the darkness that's combined with my father's cantation, it's threatening not only you, but other volcanoes across the continent?" Again, they bowed in acknowledgment. "What does that mean?"

"It means you must not lose this fight. If you do, we will return to our wild state. The people of Dóiteán will no longer be able to connect with us," Dearg said.

"And therefore, danger will be more imminent," Dubh added.

"How do we win? How do we defeat it?" I asked, the fear inside me rising now as the reality became even clearer.

"We are not sure," Gael said, as she returned to her human form of a small, dark-skinned woman with bright white hair. "You must figure this out on your own. What we are sure of is that your path must be walked together as a team. Only in that way can you defeat the darkness."

"Why?" Kyle asked. "I mean, I get it, together we fight to destroy the enemy, but how does being together help?"

Dubh responded. *"We believe it is because of your father's curse. When his cantation lost the battle with your brothers, it began to seek out any imbalance, any darkness that would embrace it. Unfortunately, the chaos that exists naturally around us was the closest and easiest for him to embrace."*

"So, this is still my father's fault," Kyle said, sounding more frustrated and annoyed than angry.

Gael looked sad. "We are connected to the chaos, therefore, we are connected to the darkness in a way you may not understand." She looked at the other two dragons before she continued. "I think your father regrets what he has done. I believe he has regretted it for some time, but he is no longer in control. His anger, even though misplaced when he cursed you, split his being. His personality, I think you'd say, became its own entity, and through the years, it's fed off you and your brothers' agony and loss. Now that your brothers have found their life partners, which in effect broke the curse against them, that dark part of your father–his cantation–grows weak and desperate."

"Why hasn't it attacked me like it did my brothers?" Kyle asked.

Gael reached out and touched his chest, smiling. "Oh, it has. You forget the barbs it injected in both your and Conley's chest. Your grandmother was able to remove it completely from you, but it has delayed your progress. It still threatens you, will always threaten you until you banish it from yours lands and ours."

Kyle sighed, and I automatically took his hand, sharing his frustration. "Don't despair, Kyle. We will overcome the darkness. My people, they can help. It's time we implore them to do what they all came to Dóiteán to do. We will banish the dark and free my friends," I said, waving toward the three dragons.

Gael smiled at me and shifted back into her dragon form. *"Then wake up and prepare for battle."*

TWENTY-SEVEN

KYLE

I WOKE UP IN the Dóiteán clinic with Conley snuggled into my side. I shook him gently, whispering, "Baby, wake up."

He shifted and blinked at me. "We were dreaming," he said quietly, mimicking my whisper.

"Apparently, but we're together. How did that happen?"

I heard a chuckle as Conley's grandmother, Mohini, came through the doorway, just in time to overhear me. "That happened when both of you collapsed in a pile on the floor and then refused to be separated. We had no choice but to put you together."

Dr. Gonzales followed her into the room along with Mr. Cho. "We could tell you were both in the same dream walk and needed to be together," Mr. Cho confirmed. "But your grandmother is correct, you refused to let each other go."

We both sat up to communicate better. "My parents?" Conley asked his grandmother.

"They are ashamed, as they should be," Mohini said. "They want to see you, but we felt it best they kept their distance until you woke up and recovered."

Dr. Gonzales came over and used her stethoscope to listen to our hearts. "You've fully recovered. That's... well, that required more than modern medicine."

"It required more than we could have done," Mr. Cho explained.

Conley nodded. "Kyle's grandmother was able to heal us. But, we come with news. Not good news, Mr. Cho. We are at war. There is..." He looked at me, then back to the group. "There's a darkness threatening the entire village, but it threatens so much more than that. It seems to be trying to force the dragons to release their fire."

Mr. Cho looked concerned. "We've felt it, young man. For quite some time, we've felt it. What do you know?"

I sat silently, letting Conley explain what we'd learned. I appreciated that he left out my father's cursed cantation, as well as our lovemaking, but I interrupted him as he skimmed that part. It was important they be fully informed about what we were really facing.

I patted Conley's hand, letting him know I was going to tell that part myself. "There's more that you need to know, and it's relevant. My father... when I was young, my father cursed my brothers and me. The curse has been following us all our lives. My brothers succeeded in overcoming the curse, which weakened it, but the dragons told us that as it has joined forces with the chaos trying to disrupt the balance Dóiteán has established."

"That explains why we haven't been successful in stemming the tide," Mohini said. "Did the dragons say how to defeat it?"

"They don't seem to know the answer," Conley said. "Just that it involves both Kyle and me."

"We were sent back here to prepare for battle," I added, wanting to emphasize the importance of this bit. "You should rally the troops as they are, and we should discuss how to help balance this out, maybe push the chaos laced with my father's curse back, at least far enough to keep things from getting out of hand."

Mr. Cho nodded. "Then you should join us this evening since we're meeting on that very topic," he said.

"And you should go to your parents' house," Mohini said to Conley, then looked at me. "You must not let family rivalry keep us from our goal. Besides, I'm sure they've learned a valuable lesson since last you visited, Kyle."

I hoped so, since I didn't want a repeat of last time, but I did resolve not to lose my temper, no matter how nasty they got. At worst, I'd just leave again.

We walked hand in hand down the road between the clinic and Conley's parents' home. "Are you nervous?" I asked as yet another passing villager looked at us with concern.

"Yes, of course. I don't want them to act foolish again, but at the same time, I think Grandma is correct. We need to clean this up to keep their negative energy from disrupting the work we have to do."

I linked my arm with his as we walked up to their garden gate.

"Want me to wait here?" I asked before we climbed the steps.

"No, we need to do this as a united front. I've never had to confront my parents before, at least not in a way that I ever won. I have to win this one, no matter what their reaction."

I stopped him before we went in. "Conley, I-I don't know how to break this to you, but if they can't accept this, we should tell them they can go stay in Chemeketa until this is over. I know a lot of people over there who would host them, but they can't be here, not if they're harboring anger."

I heard movement to my right then and turned to see Mr. Bolcan, Conley's father, come around the corner of the house. Both of us tensed at his presence. "That won't be necessary," his father said, clearly having overheard our conversation.

"Come into our home, please. Conley's mother and I have some apologizing to do."

Groveling more like, I thought, but kept that to myself.

This time when I entered their home, the air felt different. More welcoming. Even with my poor health before, I realized now what I'd felt as I walked in was animosity. This was certainly an improvement.

"Please, come to the back room," Mr. Bolcan said, and led us through the house.

Conley cocked an eyebrow. "They never entertain guests back here," he whispered, so his father couldn't hear.

He was interrupted from saying more as we rounded the corner and saw his mother standing in what looked to be the entrance to their kitchen. She looked older than before, and big bags that hadn't been under her eyes seemed to have taken up residence there. I couldn't help feeling sorry for her—an emotion I wasn't prepared to feel for either of Conley's parents, at least not yet.

"Please, come into the family room," Mr. Bolcan said, and led the way into a beautiful room filled with dark wood, exquisite antique rugs, and comfortable leather furniture. It looked like something out of a magazine.

I sat next to Conley on a wide leather sofa while both Mr. and Mrs. Bolcan sat across from us in matching leather recliners. Conley's hand hadn't left mine, and I sure as hell wasn't going to move mine from his. I could tell this was him making his boundaries known to his parents.

"We've got much to apologize for, to both of you," Mr. Bolcan began. "Mr. Franklyn, we have never treated anyone with such disrespect in our home. After Dearg made her feelings known about our reception of you, we realized just how out of line we were."

Mrs. Bolcan sat up and, wiping a tear, said, "We were both so angry. It doesn't even make sense now, how unnaturally angry we felt."

A lightbulb went off in my head. "Can you tell me more about that? Do you usually get angry like that?" I asked.

They both looked taken aback by my question, then shook their heads. "We admit, we are a bit overprotective of Conley," his father said. "He is our only child. The dragons came to us and told us we would have a child, even though we were both older and had given up hope. They said he would be strong and special. It was our duty to protect him, because there were forces that would want to destroy him."

"That's why you've always smothered me?" Conley asked, and I could feel his anger rising. "Why didn't you just tell me this instead of..."

I patted his hand, asking him to pause that thought for a moment. "I believe I may understand now a bit more of why you responded the way you did."

I explained how my father's cantation had attacked us both—Conley as he came through my side of the portal, and me when I came through this side. "My father's curse has apparently split his personality in half, creating a dark entity that's been stalking my brothers and me all our lives. We were told his darkness is now connected to the chaos energy that wants to destroy the connection between the dragons and Dóiteán. By possessing you, causing you to reject me, I'm guessing it was my father's cantation's effort to create a rift between Conley and me."

Conley's parents nodded, before his mother said, "I think you are letting us off easy, giving us a reason... an excuse. Something we can't explain did come over us, so what you said is true, but we should've resisted it. We should've been able to see it for what it was."

"Did you think I was a threat to Conley?" I asked.

Both of his parents looked embarrassed and nodded. "Then you were reacting in good faith. I've been manipulated by my father's curse ever since he cast it. I've been blinded to love in most forms. Our poor grandmother's love for us was the only thing that got through to me and my brothers. So, I can't blame you for being caught under its spell."

I saw relief pass over both of their faces. "Mr. Franklyn... Kyle, we are both so sorry and thank you for your generous spirit of forgiveness. We are both committed to earning it."

Conley suddenly dropped my hand and walked stiffly over to the window. "I'm not feeling quite as forgiving. I'm sorry, Mama, Dad, but my entire life, even as an adult, you've kept me under such a tight rein, I've barely been able to breathe. I couldn't even be with Kyle, my boyfriend, without the dragons sweeping us away from here, from you, so we could be together."

I watched as Mr. Bolcan's face flashed with anger, which he admirably quashed. I'm sure my dad, even before he became the man who could curse his children, wouldn't have handled things that well.

"We've made a lot of mistakes," his mother said. "I won't pretend I regret being protective of you, and if I'm honest, I'd make the same mistakes again if it meant keeping you safe." She looked over at her husband, then back at Conley.

"You have to understand how much we love you, how thankful we've both been to have you in our lives, especially at the age we were when you came to us."

She rose to stand next to Conley, laying her hand on his arm. "If I could undo anything, it would be how we've held onto you so hard after you became a man, not letting you go or spread your wings. Both of us..." she said, looking back at a remorseful Mr. Bolcan, "...knew what we were doing was too much. We used the excuse that the dragons wanted us to keep you safe, but honestly, we knew what the real reasons were."

Mr. Bolcan stood up and joined them. "We just love you so much, son, and we let that impede our common sense. I'm not sure you can or even want to forgive us, but if it helps, know that everything we've done was because we love you almost more than our hearts can bear."

"I thought you didn't believe in me," Conley said, and his own tears began to streak down his face. "I thought you believed me to be weak, useless."

"No!" both his parents said at once. "No, it's the opposite, you were so strong, always so strong. Power radiated from you. Even as a child you could draw up the fire so quickly and easily, it scared us. You are a child of the dragons," Mr. Bolcan said, and Conley's eyes grew large.

"What did you call me?" he asked, stunned.

Mr. Bolcan reached out and laid a hand on his son's shoulder, looking him in the eyes as he spoke. "You know what I said, Conley, you are a child of the dragons. Why are you surprised? They've actively been a part of your life, each of them at different times, but all of them involved. No other child in the history of Dóiteán has had that kind of connection. Even your vision quest seemed unnecessary, even though it was time. Why go on a vision quest with the entities that have been active participants in your life since birth?"

"That's why you allowed me to resist?"

They both nodded. "And then you were gone so long, a full year with no contact, we were both devastated, afraid...."

"They did it to try to cut the apron strings," I said to myself, and all three people turned to me. I blushed, ashamed I'd said that out loud.

Mr. Bolcan sighed. "I suppose that's exactly what the dragons were trying to do. Yet, we still didn't learn."

I stood and faced them. "If it helps, your love for Conley gives me a vision of what a real love between children and their parents can be. It's the opposite of what my brothers and I endured."

Mrs. Bolcan came over and pulled me into a hug. "I'm so sorry, Kyle, but now, you are part of our family, and despite our less than stellar beginnings, we are here for you, no matter what happens between you and our Conley."

I smiled at that and let my arm rest on the much shorter woman's shoulder. "But, minus the overprotective stuff, right?"

She nudged me and laughed. "No guarantees. As you can see, once we embrace a son, we hold on tightly."

"I think I can be okay with that." And I could, not that I expected them to adopt me.

The cursory acceptance into their family was nice, but premature, I thought. At least their kindness had shown through, though, and I was able to understand their reaction hadn't been entirely their own... just one more casualty of a curse no father should've ever cast upon his children.

Twenty-Eight

—.—

Conley

C LEARING THE AIR NEEDED to be done on all fronts. I knew as I sat there listening to my parents apologize for how they'd treated Kyle, it hadn't explained how they had treated me.

Something inside me said it was important we resolve all our issues and to do it now. Any negativity, especially in my relationship with my parents, could give ammunition to the darkness as we prepared to do battle.

How they handled it so well still shocked me. The fact they could admit they were overbearing, but that they did it out of love, well, I could feel the truth in what they were saying... that helped.

Of course, the most powerful aspect of that conversation, at least for me, was hearing for the first time that they believed in me. They didn't see me as the weakling loser I always thought they had. In fact, the opposite was true. They feared for my safety because of the gifts bestowed on me. That, all of that, was healing and exactly what I needed before we went into battle. Even if I couldn't quite admit, even to myself, that I had much power, and certainly not enough to be the child of the dragons, as they'd called me. All in all, it just felt good that they believed in me.

That night at the council meeting, we spoke with the village leaders and brainstormed ways to shore up the defenses against the encroaching darkness. They all agreed to go out and talk to their villages to discuss how best to meet those needs, and reconvene later in the week with definitive plans.

While the village leaders met with their counterparts, Kyle, Dad, Mr. Cho, Grandma, and I all went together to each component of this community, speaking with people about how best they could help us overcome the darkness.

There were eleven different groups within our community. Each of them had distinct responsibilities, mostly keeping our village operating, but also in our overall mission regarding the dragons.

The night we all reconvened, the news felt grim. Almost every group returned with more or less the same conclusion: *We don't have the capacity to put more into our efforts*.

"Why don't you invite the Chemeketa community to help?" Kyle asked, and the entire council stopped talking at once and turned toward him. "I know it's not ideal, and the leader of the Kels–those who guard the portal–has made clear the dangers of people being aware of the portal, but it seems this may be an emergency. We can use all the help we can get, right?" he asked.

That prompted a spirited discussion, which Mr. Cho allowed for a while before banging his gavel to regain control of the meeting. "Let there be a discussion on the floor now. Officially, what do we say to the suggestion Mr. Franklyn has offered?"

For a moment it seemed as if no one was going to answer. Finally, Langley stood, and said, "The people of Chemeketa are noble. They are loyal to our craft and work to balance the elements in their dimension. As someone who has had ongoing interactions with them, I stand with Mr. Franklyn's recommendation. We should, in fact, extend an invitation."

After that, many people responded, not all in favor. The Security Force, whose primary duty was to monitor our side of the portal, expressed grave concerns about opening it to such a large group of unknown individuals. "It's never been used for that purpose before," Mrs. Brighton, head of the Security Force, stated.

Once she conceded that she had no reason to think it couldn't be done, she said she'd support the council's decision either way. And if it was in favor of bringing the Chemeketa people over to help, she'd do what she could to ensure they crossed safely.

The council approved Kyle's recommendation in a unanimous decision. Only three members abstained from voting, which I thought was out of fear of something new or different happening.

"Mr. Franklyn, because you were the one to propose this offer, and because you are from that dimension, would you take our request for support to the people of Chemeketa?" Mr. Cho asked.

"Of course," Kyle agreed.

"Then please do so immediately, as we all fear how quickly things are ramping up, and we could use all the help we can get to pull the threat back."

"Conley," Kyle said, turning to me, "...if you agree to come with me, we can leave tonight. But before we go, we must ask that your healers help protect us as we cross through the portal. Neither of us wants a repeat of what happened before."

I nodded and Mr. Cho agreed and also confirmed they would ensure the portal was secured for when the volunteers from Chemeketa returned, protecting everyone from any sort of similar attack by the darkness.

When the meeting concluded, Kyle and I made short work of preparing for our journey. I still hadn't unpacked my bag from when I'd returned last time, so I simply went through it to ensure I had clean clothes, then helped Kyle repack his belongings at the clinic. Before long, we were once again headed up the mountain toward the portal that took us back into Kyle's world.

Twenty-Nine

Kyle

"Lance, I know this is extreme, but the volcanoes that Dóiteán protects are all in danger of erupting."

Katan Manning, Lance's mentor and Chemeketa's former mayor, nodded. "There is a precedent for this. When Luna Raven first arrived in Chemeketa, she appealed to the newly formed council for help, and the entire village leadership of the time came together to help her create the portal. It is completely appropriate to ask for help again now."

Katan looked over at Lance and blanched. "If you feel it would be appropriate, Mayor Franklyn," he added. Of course, Lance just smiled.

"I appreciate your input, Mayor Manning, and I don't disagree. Let's take it to the council for a vote, but before we do, Edward, as the Kels have been guardians of the portal all these years, do you have an opinion?"

He shook his head. "No, we have always known the portal to Dóiteán was as much a part of keeping this side of the dimension safe as it was to keep them safe. If they are requesting assistance, the Kels will do what we can to support them."

"Can you keep the darkness from attacking those who come through the portal, or vice versa?" I asked.

"Maybe," Edward said. "It is weaker now, so it's possible we could do so just through our people, but if the ancestors are willing to help, I feel confident we can keep all who enter or exit the portal safe."

"So be it, then," Lance said decisively. "Katan, I think you should call the council to order. I'm still too new to command your level of authority, and with something as important as this, I believe we'll need to appear as a unified force."

Katan nodded. "I think we should do it together, son. As I've said time and again, the people of Chemeketa are not the same as those you've led before. We know our calling, and you are our chosen leader, new or not."

I could tell that resonated with my brother, and I was glad to see him taking on the mantle of leadership in our grandmother's little village. My heart was full seeing how happy it made him.

That night at the Grange House, as the council convened, felt like a family reunion. Along with Lance and Drew, my brother Crea and his fiancé Eli were there as well. My family had somehow become a foundational part of Chemeketa in a short period of time, and it felt good to be included in that, even if temporarily.

Once everyone was settled, Lance turned to me and Conley. "The floor is yours to present your request to the council."

I nodded to Conley, who explained things in detail. When he finished, Donna Rummel, leader of the Earth

Guild, asked, "So is this the same entity that attacked Lance and Drew at the festival last year?" Lance nodded, but Donna persisted. "Isn't it weaker now?"

"It is," I confirmed, "which is why it joined with the chaotic forces that threaten the volcanic region Dóiteán was created to keep subdued."

I didn't go into detail beyond that, though, knowing this decision was more about ensuring the people of Chemeketa realized the danger we all faced.

"What exactly are we being asked to do?" Donna asked.

"We're a small set of villages. In total we're just a fraction larger than Chemeketa," Conley said. "We are also isolated. The nearest community to us is in South America, near what you call Peru." He shook his head. "We don't have reinforcements, no one to call on when we have a crisis. Up until now, we haven't needed help. There was no reason to need it, but now we are in danger of losing control. We need help, and the most logical source of help would be your community."

That seemed to satisfy Donna, who said, "I'm willing to state the Earth Guild would get behind this level of support. I have no doubt our Guild would be willing to cross into Dóiteán."

Lance then looked to Drew, who nodded to him from the audience, before saying, "Drew and I are willing to go as well, although the rest of the Air Guild may not be able. Also, Edward was unable to attend tonight's meeting, but he informed us the Kels can and will join in the fight."

Donna nodded. "We should reach out to our communities outside Chemeketa to enlist others. Our elderly

Guild members may not be able to handle this, and much of Chemeketa is older than me. As it is, the Earth and Water Guilds really are the strongest elements here in Chemeketa, except of course for the Kels."

"The Water Guild will help," Abigail Scott, leader of that Guild, said.

"So, let's vote," Lance said, and, of course, every council member voted in favor. "Now for the recruits. Conley, do you have an idea of how many people you'd need to hold back the dark forces that threaten Dóiteán?"

He nodded. "A hundred would help, depending on their gifts, but even more may be needed. Right now, it's hard to be specific."

Lance looked to Katan. "I'd rather err on the side of too many than too few, given what we are facing. Do we have that many people who are strong enough to travel?"

Katan shrugged. "In the village, no, but within the larger community, very likely. We won't know until we send out the call."

"Tell them there's no time to waste," I said. "The structures working to keep things balanced in Dóiteán are stretched thin. I'm sure our father's cantation is pushing things harder in the hope we can't make it in time."

"Understood," Lance said. "Okay, let's get to work."

Over the next few days, more and more people alerted us that they could and would come to Dóiteán to help. The first wave of people were scheduled to move through the portal on Saturday. "Can Grandma get word to Dóiteán that we're coming?" I asked Lance the night he announced he had a group ready to go through.

"Maybe. Drew, can you contact Grandma?" he asked.

"Yes, she's stronger. I can feel her, although we don't try to communicate anymore. But if you want the Security Force to be prepared for the incoming group, I can let her know. She should be able to communicate with them better there than we can communicate with her here."

"Then, please do," I said to Drew. "We don't want any nasty surprises hitting our people as they move through the portal. Lance, you can alert the Kels, correct?"

Lance nodded and smiled.

Once everyone had gone, I asked him what he was smiling about.

"You," he said.

"Me? Why?" I asked.

"Well, you've always avoided responsibility. It's refreshing to see you taking it on. Leadership looks good on you."

I pushed him gently, and he laughed. "Hey, this is serious. I don't want to be responsible for anyone getting hurt because of me," I said, and Lance's face fell.

"Kyle," he said, "...can you sit down for a moment? I want to talk."

"Sure, just let me make sure Conley is squared away, then I'm all yours."

I told Conley what was going on, and bless him, I could tell he was wiped out. "Hey, go on to bed. I'll be up soon," I said, and his lack of argument told me I was right.

I slipped back downstairs, and wasn't surprised to see Crea sitting next to Lance, waiting for me. Lance sighed when I sat down, and said, "So, hey, since we broke my curse against Dad, I've been seeing things more clearly.

I... well, Kyle, I just wanted to tell you how sorry I am for..."

I stopped him midsentence. "Hey, no, we were kids. You were just a teenager and so was Crea." I hesitated a moment, then after taking a deep breath and letting it out slowly, admitted, "I always blamed myself, Lance, not you, not either of you. I think I knew deep down that Dad was going to react like he did. He was different after Grandpa Franklyn died... he became colder, like Mom. They were our parents and I wanted them to know about me, but I could've predicted their reactions too. I shouldn't have set you both up like that."

"That's bullshit, Kyle," Lance said. "Dad did what he did, and that's not on any of us."

"No, it's not," Crea agreed. "It's Dad and Mom's fault. They were the adults."

"Exactly," I said as I began to get choked up. "It's not on any of us. Even the curse you cast against him, the one Crea and I gave strength to, wasn't something that would've happened if Dad had been acting like a dad, or even just an adult."

The three of us sat in silence for a while, then Crea said, "When this is done, I plan to go find him and find out what the hell was really going on with him."

Lance and I looked at him, the concern clear on our faces. "You sure that's wise?" Lance asked.

Crea shrugged. "I'm not sure of anything anymore, but I want to know. I never told you, but I confronted Mom a few years back, and she ranted on and on about my sexuality being a sin. But the truth is, I don't think she's capable of love, not really. I sensed something inside her wasn't right even then. Something was off with her."

"Psychopath," Lance said, and both Crea and I nodded.

"I think more narcissist," Crea said. "She's probably incapable of feeling empathy. She can only focus on the things she wants."

"I don't really remember her that much, if I'm honest," I said, and shook my head. "Mom was mostly absent from my life, but Dad was there, at least until his dad died."

I looked from one brother to another, and both were nodding.

"So, what happened?" I asked. "Why did he change?"

"My guess," Lance said, "...is he lost his footing after losing Grandpa. Up until then, he'd practically been Grandpa's shadow. That's why we visited Chemeketa so much, they were basically best friends. When Grandpa died, maybe Dad didn't know who he was without him, or how to find his own place in the world."

"So, he went to Mom's family? Why did he turn away from Grandma?"

"The dark side," Lance said, shaking his head. "Mom's family can be very persuasive. I didn't tell you, but they hounded me for years to renounce my sexuality and become their heir."

I laughed. "Oh, they made me the same offer, but Gods help us, I'd rather throw myself into a volcano than be around them, much less be under their thumb."

Crea sighed. "They asked me repeatedly to visit their home. I never went, always telling them I lived too far away, and I'm glad I had that easy excuse. I honestly have no interest in being around our mother again. That and, well, her parents are really awful. I couldn't stand to be around them even when we were kids."

"Why would you? They terrorized us," Lance said, his nose wrinkled in disgust. "Ugh, do you remember when they made us wear those German-looking clothes? My gods, we're Irish, a little Scottish... what was it with the German stuff?"

Crea cringed. "It was because they wanted to open a chain store in Leavenworth, up in Washington. They were saying projecting a German heritage would be more appropriate, given the town's Bavarian village theme."

I had to smile at that. "Hey, I don't know. I liked the lederhosen."

"Ugh, you would," Lance said, and laughed when I flipped him off.

"I have a thing for men in traditional clothing."

"You have a thing for men," Crea said, and laughed when I swiped at him with the back of my hand.

We all leaned back on the sofa and stared at the fireplace. "I'm glad we ended the curse against Dad. It was really a curse against us too."

"Yeah, me too," Crea said, and Lance nodded.

"It feels like we have each other back again. Whatever it was that made me want to avoid you all... it's gone," Lance said.

"Same," I said, and Crea confirmed it.

"So, now we can be family again, but let's keep it just to us brothers, okay? Not Mom and her psycho parents."

"And not Dad?" Crea asked.

Lance and I both shook our heads. "Forgiving Dad may be important, eventually, but after what he did, I can't see him ever being a part of my life again," I said.

"Agreed, but we still have to get you through all this," Lance said. "And Saturday, when we go through the portal, that's what we'll do. Get you through it."

"Get me *and Conley* through it," I said, and got cocked eyebrows from them both. "Yeah, before you get all weird, I like him. I like him a lot."

THIRTY

CONLEY

KYLE AND I STAYED back as the first wave of people walked into the cave that led to the portal to Dóiteán. Crea, Eli, Jennie, and her girlfriend Scarlett, as well as Scarlett's parents, all went through in the first group.

Eli's godparents, who he introduced to me as Lee and Indigo Chelsea, were in the first wave too, taking with them a huge contingency of hedge witches. The power coming off them reassured me and, if I was being honest, scared me a bit too. We weren't used to such powerful Earth magic in Dóiteán. I just hoped we were making the right decision.

But then, what other choice did we have?

Drew confirmed that Gwen, in her spirit form, could contact and relay the details of the crossing to Mrs. Brighton to ensure the Security Force would be there to prevent an attack as the Chemeketa folks crossed the portal. It was agreed there would be no need to involve Gwen again now that we were organized.

There would be three official waves, each crossing three days apart. We had well over a hundred people volunteer to help, and more were possible, Katan thought, as more of the energy community learned of our needs. As such, Lance and Katan convinced Kyle and me to stay back for now, to keep things moving and answer questions from the newcomers. We would be joining Lance and Drew in the second wave.

The night of the first crossing, I dreamed I was in Dóiteán.

I looked over and saw Dearg, and knew she'd brought me here to see our progress. Kyle came up behind me and took my hand. "Seems like it's working out okay," he said as we watched the groups that ran Dóiteán talk with and help organize the Chemeketa support.

Mr. Cho walked past us at one point and stopped, looking at where we stood, and squinted. "Conley, Kyle, is that you?" he asked, and smiled. "If so, it's going well. We look forward to the next wave, and the citizens of Dóiteán are putting everyone up. You did well, boys, really, really well." He then turned toward a group who'd just called him over.

"What do you think?" I asked Kyle. "Is this going to work?"

"There's no way to know, really, but at least we have some hope, and that's more than we had before."

"True," I said, and leaned into him. "Hey, wanna see if Dearg will transport us back to the hot springs? I think I'd like to try that place out again."

Kyle pulled me into his arms, turned back toward Dearg, and said, "Whattaya say? One more night at the springs before the war starts?"

I could hear Dearg chuckling, and just like that, we were both naked in the springs. "It still feels strange that she's lurking around while we're... you know."

"I don't think she gives a damn what we do, but if you don't want to... "

"Fuck that," I said, surprising myself with my foul mouth. I could feel my mother chastising me, and had to shake her voice out of my head. "I'm not going to pass up an opportunity to be alone with you, especially on the eve of battle."

"Agreed," Kyle said. He began kissing up my neck, and before I knew what was happening, I moaned and let my true feelings slip.

"Oh, my gods, I love you so much." Kyle froze, and it was only then that I realized what I'd said. "Wait, I was... "

Kyle put his finger over my mouth, smiled, and leaned in for a kiss. "I love you too," he whispered.

Thirty-One

Kyle

Conley, Lance, Drew, and I all went with the second wave of troops, as I was beginning to think of them, although our valiant volunteers were mostly people in their sixties and above. We certainly weren't a typical army, but as I walked into the village, the energy around me buzzed, sending electrical sparks through me. No, we weren't typical, but we were armed to the teeth.

The commotion helped me stay focused, otherwise my mind would've been swimming with Conley's admission the night before. *Love.* What a strange concept. Until recently, I didn't think I even knew what it was, but when Conley slipped and told me he loved me, I knew without hesitation I felt the same way. Strangely, that revelation didn't scare me. In fact, it just felt right, like it was meant to be.

"Kyle, come help!" Crea called to me from where the Earth Guild was working. "Can you help with the natural gas well we found?" Just like that, I was drawn into the fray.

Different segments of Dóiteán, all fire energies who had worked to calm the dragons in various ways, were paired for the first time with the other three elements to ensure an eruption wouldn't occur.

It was a remarkable moment in time. Each night, after the groups had done what they could to alleviate the pressure, Mr. Cho, Lance, Mr. Bolcan, Conley, and I would get together to assess the pressure levels in the three dragons.

Nothing we were doing seemed to be working.

"What do you think is happening?" I asked, frustrated. "Basic physics dictates that as we remove the causes of the pressure, such as the gasses underground, the pressure inside the mountains should subside."

"Unless it's the lava flow itself. If it is pushing up from underground, wouldn't that be reason enough for the mountains to erupt?" Conley asked.

"Yes, but we've checked that. The lava hasn't moved in months, and in Dubh, it's been years," I argued.

"So, the pressure is coming from something else."

I looked out the window toward where the darkness, like a storm cloud, loomed and hung around the three mountains. "It's that," I said, shaking my head. "It's somehow pressurizing them. Somehow we have to push the darkness back."

"Isn't your relationship with Conley doing that?" Lance asked.

I shook my head. "Obviously not. We're clearly together, and it continues to get stronger," I said, and took Conley's hand in mine. "But, somehow, unlike you and Crea, it's not enough."

"What about the ruby?" Drew asked as he came into the room and sat down next to Lance.

"What ruby?" I asked, confused.

"The one your grandmother gave you, one of the stones from her ring. The diamond was given to Lance. The emerald to Crea. You got the ruby."

I reached underneath my shirt and felt for the ruby necklace. I'd gotten so used to wearing the pendant, I didn't even notice it any longer. "Yeah, what about it?" I asked.

"The diamond transformed when Lance and I accepted our love for one another. The same happened for Crea and Eli. They became tattoos that glow when our love is expressed," he said, pointing to a faint diamond-shaped tattoo on his forehead.

I shook my head and pulled the ruby out from my shirt so everyone could see it. "This one's done nothing."

"So, that means we're missing something," Drew said. "If you and Conley's relationship is what we need to defeat the darkness, or at least push it back, then it should work, shouldn't it?"

I looked at the group, then over at Conley. "Yeah, in theory. But, the entity was stronger when it fought you, and it wasn't woven into the chaos that keeps wanting to unbalance the dragons. I'm not sure it will work the same as it did for you two."

Drew shrugged, but I could tell he didn't believe that. Maybe I didn't either. Was it possible Conley wasn't the one I was supposed to be with?

No, that was preposterous. Seriously, the dragons themselves fixed us up. My grandmother was pulling strings from the other side of the veil, for goodness' sake, to make things work between us. But what if Drew was right and the ruby wasn't reacting, because something between us was off?

That night as Conley lay in my arms, I stared up at the ceiling, wondering. Should I be doing something else? Should I be trying to get Conley to do something else? But no matter how long or hard I thought about it, I couldn't wrap my mind around what that could possibly be.

The next day, I continued working where I was needed. Conley spent most of his time trying to communicate with the dragons, but they weren't much help either. One full week passed, and things were not improving.

Once again, we met with the group leaders. "So, what if we provided a different outlet? Something away from the large volcanoes where the pressure could be alleviated. It's always been a theory that volcanoes, at least in the same region, are linked. The fact that the pressure is building in each of the three dragons seems to indicate that theory is correct, so why can't we do that?" Conley asked.

"Like what? A fourth volcano? You want us to create a baby volcano?" I asked, concerned about what that would look like, let alone the danger involved.

He shrugged. "Yeah, why not? The biggest threat is that the mountains will explode like Gael did. That's what caused all the ash in the atmosphere, not to mention the lahars and the floods. What if there were no glaciers to create any floods?"

I thought for a moment about what he was proposing. "It might work. Have you asked the dragons what they think?" I asked.

He shook his head. "No, I just thought of it, but I think we should ask. Maybe we should ask them together."

I smiled. I'd been wondering since last week if I should be trying to give Conley more space. Maybe I wasn't supposed to be with him. No matter how ridiculous that sounded, now that the thought was in my head, I couldn't quite drive it out.

Maybe it was because I'd spent a lifetime losing the people I loved, but it seemed like I was just setting myself up for the same thing. Now that I'd opened my heart to Conley, I knew eventually I'd be so deeply in love with him, that losing him would be excruciating. Sort of like having something pierce your real heart.

That night, Conley asked a hundred and one questions about volcanism. How the physics worked, how pressure could be diverted away from one, or in this case, three volcanoes to a new one. Where would the new one go? Could it be built so it didn't create problems for civilization, either in Dóiteán or on my side of the portal?

Mostly, I didn't have answers. Each question had so many different facets to consider. Ultimately, my concern was that we were playing with natural and spiritual forces so far beyond what humans or even our gifted ancestors could or even should attempt to control.

Unable to sleep, I finally got up and walked downstairs. We were staying with Mr. Cho and Conley's grandmother, because, well, Conley hadn't been comfortable sleeping with me in his parents' house, even after they apologized for being angry.

The fire in the fireplace was banked and gave off a warm glow. As I sat staring into the fire, I felt myself slowly drifting off.

I was standing in the meadow once again. Grandma was there, and I could see the dragons flying overhead. Just the way they were moving told me they were anxious and concerned.

"What am I supposed to do to stop this?" I asked her.

She smiled at me. "Love, no matter who you fall in love with, comes with sacrifice."

I nodded. "So, what is that sacrifice? Am I supposed to jump into an active lava flow?"

"You were always so dramatic. No, and I have no idea as to the necessary sacrifice. All I know is that's the message I've gotten repeatedly as I've searched for the answers to help you."

I glanced up at the darkness that now looked like black smoke pushing against the three dragons' defenses.

"I'm not even sure what all this means. I mean, I've given up my fears about being in a relationship. I've let Conley in, and in a way I've never done before. What other sacrifice would I have to make?"

She shrugged sadly. "Grandson, I don't have answers, except what I've said."

She and I stood quietly looking up at the dark before she said, "The idea Conley had about the new volcano is a good one. It might be the key to shifting all of that—" She waved toward the sky. "—into something else. Something less dangerous."

I nodded. "I think so too. I'll talk with Yvonne tomorrow. She's here and might have an idea how to make this work... If we can make it work."

She patted my hand and smiled. "You'll make it work. For what it's worth, I can feel that."

I woke up in the sitting room, staring into the fire again. My grandmother's faith in me was worth a lot. It was worth everything, especially considering that for much of my life, I had such little faith in myself.

Dawn had already broken over the horizon, and I could hear life beginning to stir in the house, so I went upstairs, changed quietly so as not to disturb Conley, and went over to the cottage where Yvonne and Sammy were staying.

Yvonne was always an early riser, and I was happy to find her sitting on the cottage's front stoop, coffee in hand. "Hey, thought I might find you here," I said, startling her.

"Hey, yourself," she said, smiling.

"So, I have questions," I said, and her smile brightened.

"Well, what else is new?" she asked, and I slipped onto the stoop next to her.

She bumped my shoulder, which knocked a frustrated sigh out of me.

"Okay, that bad, huh?" she asked.

I shook my head. "Yvonne, what we're doing should be working, but it's not. I've wracked my brain, and Dóiteán, with all of our help, has done miraculous things... it should be working."

She nodded. "It should be, in theory."

"But, I think we're all in agreement. The darkness, the chaos linked to my dad's hatred, seems to be creating its own form of pressure."

I stared toward the three mountains in the distance and sighed again. "I had a vision last night and saw my grandmother."

"Wow, okay, like when she teleported you?" she asked.

"Well, sort of, it's happened a lot since I met Conley, but no, she hasn't teleported me lately. It feels a bit mundane at this point."

Yvonne was looking at me strangely, but didn't respond. "Anyway, I saw the mountains manifested as dragons... that's a long story, and beside the point, but they were anxious. I could tell they were concerned. I'm not sure how long we can hold off the inevitable."

"What have you tried?" she asked, and memories of the times she sat with me, trying to navigate the science around volcanism over the years, flashed through my mind, causing my heart to warm. Yvonne was not only a teacher, but my dearest friend. I probably should've come to her before.

"Okay..." I began, and shared all the things the community had tried, even mentioning Conley's suggestion of creating a fourth volcano and what my grandmother had said about it being a good idea.

"Well," she said after I finished speaking, "...you know I pursued science instead of the energy approach. And that was because science, even though it doesn't have a full grasp on all the powers that exist, gives us a method to follow for success."

She looked up again toward the darkness that surrounded the mountains. "Sometimes, I think science isn't able to help us, because it doesn't take into consideration the spiritual side of things."

She turned back toward me. "My dear Kyle, you've been following the scientific process, and you as well as the leaders here in Dóiteán and our Chemeketa leaders have done an excellent job with that, but since that's not working, maybe you should think outside the box."

"Like creating a new volcano?"

"Yes, but not to alleviate pressure. More to balance the darkness and the light. A beacon for all energies to flow through, thus mitigating the elements. Our magic has never required human sacrifice. But, on a spiritual level, yes, I think maybe something along those lines may be needed."

That gave me pause to think. "The question is, how would that kind of sacrifice look on a spiritual level?"

She shrugged. "I think that's what you and Conley have to figure out... together."

"Maybe," I said, more to myself than Yvonne. "And maybe we already have the answer."

I barely took the time to say goodbye before I rushed off to get Conley. If I was correct, the solution had been there the whole time.

"How fast can you pack?" I asked Conley when I dashed into the bedroom, waking him up.

"Um, I don't know," he said, wiping sleep from his eyes.

"Well, hurry. I think I have a solution, and we've got to go," I said, and rushed to grab a shower. Damn, this had to work, and Gods help us if it didn't.

Thirty-Two

Conley

I'D FELT KYLE'S RESTLESSNESS throughout the night and didn't fall asleep myself until he got up. I figured if he needed me, he'd ask. When he didn't, I finally fell into a fitful sleep plagued with nightmares of the dragon mountains exploding and the destruction of Dóiteán, Chemeketa, and the many hometowns of the people who had come to help us from the other side.

When Kyle dashed back into our room, I could tell he had a solution, or at least an idea. Anything was more than we currently had, so I couldn't help but feel excited. I thought about joining him in the shower, but I'd just heard my grandmother walk down the hallway, and decided that was probably not the best idea.

I hauled myself out of bed and brushed my teeth as Kyle busied himself getting ready. "I'm going to go down and talk to Mr. Cho and your grandmother. I think I know how to do this, at least I have a hypothesis," he said. "But pack, we need to go to the cabin... well, the meadow, but yeah... both."

I opened my mouth to ask what the meadow had to do with it, but he was gone before I got the words out. So, shaking my head, I climbed into the shower and let the warm water flow over me.

When I came downstairs, Kyle was sitting across from a concerned-looking Mr. Cho. Grandma looked downright worried, which made me think maybe what Kyle was considering wasn't the safest thing for us to do.

"Do you think you can get the community to rally behind the idea?" Kyle asked.

Both of them nodded. "No doubt, but what you're proposing, it's so dangerous," Mr. Cho said.

"So is doing nothing," Kyle said, standing up and coming over to me. "Are you packed?" I nodded. "Good, have breakfast. Your grandmother is packing us extra food to take with us, because I don't know how long this will take, but we should leave as soon as possible."

He gave me a peck on the cheek, but was gone before I could respond. "What's going on?" I asked, looking to Grandma to help me fill in the gaps.

She sighed as she finished stuffing a bag with food, apparently for the journey, before handing me a cup of coffee. "Nothing good, but maybe necessary."

Mr. Cho stood and shook my free hand. "I'll go gather the council, begin to rally the troops, but Conley, be safe, okay? You shouldn't put your life at risk unless you're absolutely sure what you're doing will work."

"What *are* we doing?" I asked, but Mr. Cho was already headed out the door. I turned to ask Grandma, but she, too, was disappearing out the back door and into the garden.

Kyle walked into the kitchen a few moments later carrying his backpack. "We should go."

"No, you should tell me what's going on," I said, feeling more than a little put out.

Kyle smiled. "I spoke with Yvonne, my professor friend, this morning. I think I know how and where to put your new volcano. I think we've been shown where to put it since we first met."

"The meadow?" I asked, and Kyle nodded.

"Think about it. All three mountains flow downward toward that meadow. It's almost as if all three are drawing energy from there already. Also, the river that runs along the edge of it, all three mountains, drain their glacial melt into that river, correct?" he asked.

I thought about it, and even Gael, who'd blasted off an entire side of her caldera, still drained into the river.

"Okay, you know where, but how?" I asked. "How do we get the darkness to flow into the meadow and not into the dragons?"

"Because we'll be there," he said.

"And you think your dad's energy will target us?" Kyle nodded again. "It's risky," I said. "What if it doesn't work? What if we piss it off and cause one or more of the dragons to erupt?"

"How likely is it that they'll erupt if we *don't* do something, and soon?" he asked.

"Point taken. Okay, let's go, but we need to figure out how to channel the energy."

"Mr. Cho is working on that. I think when we're ready, if the two combined communities focus their efforts on the meadow, we can bring up the lava there, causing the pressure to shift away from the three dragons. If there's no lava there, or even if the lava levels fall no matter what the darkness does, the volcanoes won't erupt."

"Clever, just…"

Kyle laughed and kissed me, nearly spilling my coffee. "Ask me as we're hiking. We really need to go. If for some reason this doesn't work, we need time to come up with alternatives, and I'm guessing the hike to the meadow isn't a fast one."

I nodded. "A two-day hike from here. We have to go into the dragons' territory, then between Gael and Dubh along the river."

"Good, I was hoping to spend the night in Dearg's cabin?"

I shrugged. "Maybe, if it's safe."

"Then there's no time to waste, let's go."

THIRTY-THREE

KYLE

As soon as we were beyond the village, I explained to Conley the details of my plan. "So, we need to pull the focus of the energy away from the dragons. We both agree on that point, correct?" I asked as we walked along the trail that led to the mountains.

"Yes, and you think we can do that in the meadow?" he asked.

"I'm pretty sure we can. The meadow already feels like it's a convergence where all the volcanic forces meet."

"So, you want to create a volcano in the meadow?"

"Yes, but not a huge one, just something that allows us to shift the pressure away from them and into a safer place."

"What about the other side? When we build a new volcano here, won't the same occur there?" Conley asked.

"Maybe, it's hard to say. The dragons said they don't represent just themselves, so it's possible the new volcano will be something different from them, or just another aspect of them."

We walked on for several minutes, before I added, "Think about it. This is a natural response. The people of Dóiteán, along with Chemeketa, have pulled the pressure out or away from the mountains. My dimension isn't at risk of a major earthquake, thanks to the Earth Guild's work. But, earthquakes are still happening, pressure is still rising, so it only goes to show, this isn't natural, this is... well, shit, it's my dad's cantation, Conley."

"So, what? How do we get the pressure to build under the meadow?"

"Just a simple shift of the energies."

"Simple... how is it simple?"

"I have to put myself in the way and let my dad's cantation come for me. My grandma can communicate with Dóiteán for us, so at the same time he's coming for me, the village and the dragons can be shifting the forces toward me."

Conley stopped in his tracks, eyes wide and mouth agape. "You're going to sacrifice yourself?" he asked, his voice cracking slightly.

"Only if I have to, Conley, but not necessarily. I'm not one hundred percent sure, but I don't think I have to be at the point of detonation. I think I can use this to channel the energy." I showed him the ruby pendant, and he looked confused. "This stone represents us, Conley. The love we're creating together. The very thing my dad's cantation hates the most. I believe if we place the pendant where the volcano should erupt, we can move back far enough to be safe."

"And your dad's cantation will see it as representative of us?"

I nodded, then shrugged. To be honest, I was going out on a limb here. Each time the cantation had attacked my brothers, it was our grandmother's gifts—the precious stones from her wedding ring–that had become weapons to save them. I had no doubt that would happen again.

"The ruby is our greatest weapon to use against the cantation. If we're fighting to keep the dragons from erupting, this may be all we have."

Conley didn't respond, but the look of worry marring his beautiful face spoke volumes, and we walked in silence until we were both hungry. We had just sat down to eat when the earth began to shake. We scrambled to safety and when the quake ended, Conley sighed, sounding resigned. "This is getting worse. I'm not sure your plan will work, but I do know our time is running out. I can only hope you know what you're doing, Kyle. I trust you."

Thirty-Four

Conley

As Kyle explained his plan, it became clearer in my head that what he was saying was exactly what needed to happen. The meadow, a place where I'd spent many days in my teen years and early adulthood and fell in love with Kyle in our shared dreams, seemed to be the perfect place.

Like him, I thought that was what we'd been shown from the first time we met, we just couldn't see its significance then. The meadow had been my place, and now it was *our* place. The only part of Kyle's plan that I couldn't figure my way around was his ruby and our ability to get away fast enough not to implode with it.

No, one of us would have to hold the crystal, draw the power into it, be the catalyst. I wondered how he wasn't seeing that.

"You are a child of the dragons," my dad had said.

It was beginning to make sense now. A child of the dragons, the volcanoes, would be... a new, smaller volcano.

After the earthquake, I closed my eyes. Pulling the dragons into my consciousness, I felt them connect to me in my mind.

"Are we alone? Kyle, can you hear us?"

When he didn't respond, Dearg said, "We knew you wanted to speak in confidence. Why have you called us, Conley?"

I explained Kyle's theory. I watched the dragons for confirmation, and when they didn't give any, I sighed. "So, what? This isn't what we have to do?"

"We aren't sure, not completely," Dubh said.

"But you think this might be how it has to happen. I can feel it."

The three dragons bowed in agreement. "Be honest with me, am I some child of the dragons like my parents said?"

The three dragons bowed again in affirmation. "Damn, I'm a sacrifice. I'm the damned volcano, aren't I? So, what now, I'm going to die? What about Kyle, will he die too?"

The dragons were quiet like they often were when they didn't have a response or were pondering one. "We don't have answers to your questions, Conley," Gael said. "But we do know you were chosen for this task. You and Kyle were both chosen."

"This is unfair!" I yelled at the dragons. "Why wasn't I warned? Why can't you know for sure?"

The dragons didn't respond this time, so I pulled myself back out of my dream state and found Kyle staring at me.

"You were gone for a while," he said.

"Yeah, I was checking in with the dragons. We should go."

Kyle looked at me strangely, and I could tell he had questions, but I pretended like I hadn't noticed. I wasn't ready to tell him what I believed all this meant. Not yet anyway. I needed more time to prepare myself.

Thirty-Five

Kyle

Conley grew distant after we'd stopped to eat, and he'd connected with the dragons. I knew he was feeling the pressure. The truth was, I thought I had a way to keep us both safe. Well, Conley at least.

If my brothers' experiences were any measure of what we were up against, I figured it would be a stand-off. My brothers had to fight side by side with their lovers to break the curse. I'd already decided I had to do what I could to keep Conley safe.

We walked quietly the rest of the way to Dearg's cabin. When we got there, it was a total mess. The earthquake had knocked stuff off the walls, and there was even broken glass strewn about the room where an old lamp had fallen and shattered. Unlike when we'd been here in our dream state, the place was also dirty, as if it'd been sitting vacant, and there was no food to be found.

I built a fire in the fireplace and pulled the sheets off the sofa that someone had thrown on them like dust covers. It was getting could outside; Conley warmed up water for tea.

"You going to tell me why you're so quiet?" I finally asked him.

Conley looked at me before letting out a long sigh. "Kyle, your plan, it's not complete, not as you described it. There's no way we can cause a volcano to erupt using your grandmother's ruby pendant.

"We both know that's not how this has to work."

"No, it could work. If we direct..."

Conley put his hand up to stop me. "I spoke to the dragons. Kyle, I think I'm the volcano you'll be creating."

"Wait," I said and began to pace. "You think you're supposed to sacrifice yourself and become a dragon? A freaking volcano?" I couldn't believe what he was saying, which only made me more frustrated. "No, that doesn't make sense. People don't become volcanoes. That's myth..."

Conley stood and put his hand on my arm to stop my pacing. "Listen, Kyle, I feel like my whole life—my connection to the dragons, the meadow being my safe place, meeting you—has been building to this moment. Call it destiny or not, but I really think this is the solution to our problem. I think deep down, I've always known it would be me who had to make it happen."

"That's bullshit, Conley. I didn't spend *my* whole life destined to meet you only to have you leave me like this, by sacrificing yourself. Besides, people don't become...."

"No, but people can control volcanoes... or, at least, witches with the power of fire energy can help to control them."

"So, what about me, huh?" I asked, my frustration turning to worry. "I'm as much a part of this as you are. More maybe because it's my dad's fucking curse that's causing all this to happen. So, am I supposed to become toast too so we can appease whatever deranged fire gods you're trying to appease?"

"Kyle," he said, resignation on his face. "It's not about appeasing, it's about making it happen. We need to pull the pressure off the three dragons, and we need to do it by pulling energy toward us. I'm already connected with the dragons, you aren't. There's no way to make this happen just with you."

"Nor with just you," I said and collapsed onto the sofa, causing a dust cloud to rise around me. "I'm the catalyst for my father's anger. And maybe you're the catalyst for the dragons. If there's a sacrifice, it's both of us, Conley. We're in this together."

"So, what do we do?" he asked.

Just then, the earth quaked slightly, causing the few pictures left on the wall to move. "We do what we have to," I said. "And pray it doesn't hurt too much?"

That evening we lay watching the fire, not really speaking as the uncertain reality of what we were both going to do the next day weighed heavily on us. *Together.* At least we would be facing this disaster together.

THIRTY-SIX

— · —

CONLEY

W E MADE LOVE QUIETLY that night, not bothering to go to the hot springs. I was not sure when we fell asleep, but when we woke the next morning, the sun was shining, and we could hear the birds singing in the trees outside the window.

"You okay?" Kyle asked when I finally pulled myself out of bed.

I nodded and walked over to where he stood, pulling on his t-shirt, and into his arms.

"I don't want us to die," I whispered, feeling like anything but a brave warrior.

"Me neither, maybe we won't? I mean, I don't know how we'll draw up the pressure from the volcanoes and not die, but... you know... magic?"

I chuckled, grateful he was trying to lighten the mood. "You always this optimistic?" I asked.

"Gods, no, never. I'm the world's worst pessimist. But, I want to have a long, happy life with you."

"At least we have each other, for now," I said, and wanted to cry.

"Hey, chin up. I'm not sure what's going to happen, but whatever does, it's good to have you with me. And, we are both of the fire. Maybe once we begin to pull the power to us, we can get away. So don't give up hope, not yet, okay?"

I nodded, although I had a feeling what we were going to experience would be bad. How could it not be? Even Mr. Cho, who was by far the most powerful master of the fire energy in our village, wasn't strong enough to hold off a volcano. Not even a small one.

We had instant coffee and granola bars we'd brought with us for breakfast, then headed out the door to literally face the fire. We had only walked a short distance before the darkness was there to greet us.

THIRTY-SEVEN

KYLE

"CONLEY, WHY IS IT so bad again?" I asked. "It didn't even bother us yesterday."

The moment I stepped into the dark, I choked on the heat and smoke. "Fuck, Conley are you here?" I asked, not able to see much in front of me.

My hand touched his body, though, and then I heard him coughing. He felt for my hand and through the terror, we held onto each other tightly as he drew me through the forest, on what I thought must be the path. The same path my grandmother had brought us along in the dream state.

"Grandma," I called out in my mind, *"...can you help us?"*

Immediately, she appeared in front of us, pushing the dark away, only slightly, but enough to allow us to breathe again. *"Grandma, we need to get to the meadow. Now."*

She nodded and turned away. This time as she led us, she stayed close, and I could tell she was concentrating on keeping the darkness back as we moved forward.

It seemed to take ages as we wandered around fallen trees and debris I assumed had covered the trail during the earthquakes.

Finally, just as I was beginning to think we might never get out of this horror show, I saw my grandmother begin to chant something I couldn't hear. When she began to wave her arms in a circular pattern above her head, the dark began to lift and within seconds, we were once again in our little meadow.

The darkness turned into a light mist, then disappeared altogether, and I collapsed on the ground and fought to catch my breath. "Damn," I said. "That was worse than waking through a forest fire."

Conley coughed and nodded after falling to the ground next to me. When we finally caught our breath, I looked up at my grandmother and said, *"We need you to let the villagers know we're about to start the ritual. Grandma, I love you, and if this kills us, I want you to cross the veil with us, okay?"*

She smiled sadly before she lowered her head in acceptance, then she was gone.

"She's trying to preserve her strength." I turned to see Gael standing between the other two dragons, all in their human forms.

"So, this is really happening," I said, and all three nodded.

"We've worked to keep the darkness and chaos that has wanted to attack you since you arrived here at bay, but when we are done speaking, we will leave and return to our mountain forms. We must, so we can help push the pressured forces that are plaguing us your way. But when we do, those forces will be released on you again. So be prepared," Gael said.

"Are we going to die?" Conley asked, and I put my arm around him.

Dearg nodded. "Part of you will die. It is inevitable. Any time there is change, there is death, but we are unsure what the final outcome will be. This is your destiny, not ours. And your choice to be here, with us now, has been your own. We have watched you as you have come to terms with this decision. There is no way to know what will happen, but we have done what we can to protect you. Hopefully, that will be enough."

Conley walked over and pulled Dearg into a hug, then did the same with Dubh and Gael. "You've always been my friends and my teachers. I love you, and thank you for all you've done for me."

Dubh embraced Conley the longest before he said, "We are... well, we aren't sentient, not like you, but through you and your ancestor Luna Raven, we've come to learn what it means to love. It's what has made us more human than we have ever been before. So, believe me when I say, our spirits are linked with yours. In that way, we love you and we wish you the best."

The dragons stepped back, and each began to disappear. As they faded, I could feel the power shift around us. At first, I thought it was because the dragons had left, but then I heard chanting and immediately knew it was the folks in Dóiteán.

"It's time, Conley," I said, and he turned to me.

"Are you sure?" he asked, tears now streaming down his face.

"Are you?" I asked, cupping his face in my hands, and wiping away the tears.

"Yeah, I think I am. But not here. Let's walk deeper into the meadow. I feel it's supposed to happen further away from the dragons. The baby dragon will need room."

THIRTY-EIGHT

CONLEY

D ARKNESS FLOWED AROUND US as we moved through the meadow to the far end of the valley. Anger, frustration, and hatred swirled through the air, making me more and more unsettled the further we walked.

I looked over at Kyle, who also had a look of apprehension on his face, as we forced our way through the dark.

After walking what felt like miles, we finally reached a spot just on the edge of the valley that felt right. I bent down and put my hand on the stone under me. "This is it."

"Yes, I can feel the lava flowing under us. One last time, are you sure?" he asked.

"No, but now that we're here, I know it's now or never. But, Kyle, hold me, okay?"

He nodded and took me into his arms. I could've happily stayed like that forever, if only... If only our destiny and the lives of everyone we loved didn't depend on... well, us.

After a moment, we pulled apart, but just long enough for Kyle to place the ruby pendant on the stone beneath us.

He put his hand over it, then closed his eyes. The darkness began to swirl around us, angry and full of malice. I could feel it trying to topple us, trying to push us down. It was almost as if the darkness itself had gone mad.

I quickly put my hand over Kyle's.

"I love you, Conley," he said as tears slipped down his cheek. "I love you with all my heart."

Tears sprang to my eyes too, and I leaned into him, letting our lips meet.

As we kissed, I felt the heat rising up from the pendant, pulling the lava up with it. The chanting from the villagers grew louder, as well as the sound of the dark wind swirling around us. It was almost deafening, and I had to resist the urge to put my hands over my ears.

Before I could, fire erupted below us, sending both Kyle and me into the sky, our hands still joined, and the pendant still vibrating with energy under them.

Just as I thought the volcanic forces were going to engulf and destroy us, red light began to pour out of the pendant, encircling us. I somehow ended up in Kyle's embrace as the wind swirled us around in circles and the volcano erupted beneath us.

"I love you too, Kyle," I said, and this time when we kissed, I felt the red light sear into my chest. When I looked down, I saw the ruby design tattooed there. When I looked at Kyle, he had a matching one on his chest. Both could be clearly seen through our clothing.

Still holding hands, I pulled him to me, and we kissed again, right before everything went black.

Thirty-Nine

Kyle

Fog seemed to engulf me. At least it wasn't the same dark mist that had plagued us since we'd been together.

I could sense Conley was close to me, but I couldn't see or communicate with him. I just knew we were both still together.

At first, I was afraid. But, the longer we existed in the world of mists, the more I enjoyed the freedom. It was almost as if I were the mist myself, free to move among the trees, along the ground, and into the streams that flowed around me.

I was not sure how much time passed, but eventually, I began to recognize my surroundings. First, it was the meadow, then I noticed the small cinder cone volcano erupting at the edge. *Well, that makes sense*, I thought to myself. Cinder cones were common on the sides of other larger, volcanic forces.

Not that it mattered really since clearly, I was dead. And if I was right and Conley was floating out here with me, he had apparently died in the blast as well.

The next thing I noticed was that we weren't alone. I saw my grandmother, although I couldn't get to her. She was looking at me but unable to communicate. The same was true for the dragons. They were there but not accessible.

At one point, I saw the village of Dóiteán. The villagers were in mourning. I assumed it was for Conley and... well, maybe for both of us.

I also saw my brothers, both with red-rimmed eyes and looking exhausted. *I'm so sorry, Lance, Crea,* I thought, but they couldn't see or hear me. I felt bad that we'd done so much just to lose each other in the end.

Yvonne, however, reacted differently. The moment I found myself next to her, she looked oddly in my direction, then frowned. "You need to go back to your body, Kyle. You can't continue like this if you wish to survive."

"What?" I asked, but although she clearly sensed me, she didn't seem to hear me.

Go back to my body? I doubted that was possible since even a cinder cone's energy was enough to have turned my body to ash. I figured maybe she was confused, but that really wasn't like her.

Then, energy began to pull me back over the village of Dóiteán, through the meadow and past the cinder cone volcano, which was still erupting, and along the river that still flowed violently, although less so than when Conley and I followed it the day we'd visited.

My journey ended in Dearg's cabin. The three dragons were there, in actual dragon form, as was Grandma and... was that Conley? What was he doing there?

I moved closer to get a better look and saw him kneeling over me. Over my body. "Kyle," he said, tears flowing freely down his cheeks. "Come back... come back to me..."

"He's here," I heard my grandmother tell him as she looked at me. *"Kyle, you must return to your body. You need to go back now, before it's too late."*

Her words reached out and drew me back as some part of me hovered above the physical shell I could see below.

Then, very suddenly, I opened my eyes, and I was back where I belonged, inside my own skin. "Um, what's going on?" I heard myself ask.

"You're alive!" Conley shouted, and pulled me into his arms.

"How? How are we alive?" I asked into his chest, still more confused than anything else.

Conley wiped tears as he released his tight hold of me. "We weren't there, not in our bodily form," he said, and looked to where all three dragons now stood in their human forms. "It was the dragons. They sent us to the meadow in a dream state."

"But I was dead," I said, looking first at him, then at those in the room with us. My grandmother was the first to speak.

"No, but you were in a trance we couldn't lift. One last vicious deed carried out by your dad's cantation," she said in disgust.

"His final one, I hope," I said, and she shook her head sadly.

"He's weaker and the chaos energy he was linked to has been banished. They will not be able to rebuild their forces against us."

"So, we're alive and all of that, everything we went through, was just a dream?" I asked.

"The volcanic force we created together is certainly real enough," Conley said as he pulled me into another hug. "But, yes, we're alive, thanks to the dragons."

"What about the volcano? Did it do its job?"

All three dragons nodded. "Yes, it has redirected the chaotic energy and darkness," Conley said.

I smiled, feeling relieved. "We should go back to Dóiteán and celebrate."

Conley smiled sadly but shook his head. "It's too dangerous for us to go back there now. We have to wait until we stop erupting."

"What?" I asked. "We aren't erupting."

Grandma chuckled behind us. *"Well, this is one of those times literal is better. Grandson, you and Conley are the volcano. You are what brought it into being, and even though it was your spirits that created it, it was still you. You can't go back to Dóiteán because you would literally destroy it."*

"So how are we here?" I asked.

Dearg chuckled. "You are in the cabin at the foot of my mountain. We protect it so I doubt you can do that much damage to a home protected by three large volcanic forces."

"Oh, okay," I said, but smiled. "When will the eruption end?"

"When it ends," Dubh said. "Once you let yourself go, young dragon, you have to let the forces work themselves out on their own."

"Wait, *young dragon?*"

Conley laughed. "Yeah, that shocked me too. But, we are... well, we're like them," he said as he waved his hand around the room.

"Okay, so we aren't dead, but we aren't really the same either?"

"No, dear" Grandma said as she kissed my forehead, like she used to when I was young. *"You are something more than what you were. I'll go tell everyone you're safe, but you and Conley will get to spend some quality time here in the cabin before you can return to the village. I recommend you use the time to... get to know each other better."*

She was laughing as she left, the three dragons leaving with her.

"She's right, we're stuck, and it's safer for us to be here than anywhere else," Conley said, still blushing from my grandma's comment. "Unless you want to stay in the erupting meadow?"

"Okay, I might need more information, but for now, let's follow Grandma's advice. Can we use the hot springs, or will we boil the water away?"

"No idea, but let's go find out," Conley said and stripped his shirt off as he ran out the front door.

◈

"Conley, baby, are you going to do laundry today or not?"

He slipped into the kitchen smiling like the Cheshire cat, kissed me, and dashed out the door without responding. "Hey, I know where you live!" I yelled as he disappeared down the path toward Dubh's mountain.

Gael was standing in her human form outside the door, clearly about to knock, when Conley rushed out.

"He's running from chores again?" she asked, laughing.

"Clearly, but to be honest, I just have to do one load of clothes, and then I'm done."

"Or you could do no load."

"You know we have to go back to our regular lives when this is all done, so we need to keep up the process of... well, living."

"You do what you have to do."

Gael had become a regular at our house. Dubh had become more of Conley's mentor, with the two of them touring the grounds around the now four volcanic mountains, and Conley embracing his dragon self. Dubh had told us early on that we'd have a choice once our volcano stopped erupting as to whether we returned to civilization or not. "If you wish to return, you should try to focus your energy on that life," he'd advised.

Between the two of us, Conley seemed to want the life of a dragon, while I, even after all that'd happened to me with my dad, still wanted what that life had to offer.

"Did you visit your brothers?" Gael asked as I finished tossing clothes in the washing machine.

"Yes, and thanks for helping strengthen our connection. I'm not sure why I can't seem to hold one on my own."

"It'll come with time. When we first took on our dragon form, I was completely incapable of creating a connection with humans. Dubh was the strongest among us, and he was able to communicate for all three of us. It took me many years to develop the skill."

"So, they want me to move to Chemeketa," I said, changing the subject. I wanted to see what the possibility of that was, now that Conley and I existed as dragons and as people. "Is that even possible?"

"To be honest, I'm unsure." She walked toward the window and looked out toward the cliff and the view that held her mountain in the distance. "You will have to experiment. If you try to go through the portal and are sent back, then no. If you try and succeed, then yes."

I chuckled behind her. "Thanks, that's so helpful."

She turned and smiled at me. "You know all this is new to us too, and you are part of our range, which is why there was no eruption on your side of the dimension. So, regardless of what happens, we will be here for you."

"In other words, you're family."

She nodded. "So, how will you convince Conley to leave?"

"I doubt that's a real possibility, but since we can use this dream state to live together, I can have a life there and one with him here. It's the best of all worlds."

"I agree," Dearg said, startling me.

"Ugh," I grumbled, "are you ever going to stop with that?"

"Nope, I like watching you jump like a jackrabbit."

This was a typical day for us. The dragons had become more human since we'd arrived. Well, at least Dearg and Gael had. Dubh seemed to prefer his dragon form, which was the same for Conley lately. I knew by now he and Dubh were somewhere up in the sky, flying around enjoying the view.

To be honest, I enjoyed that too. A lot actually, but I wanted more. I wanted to get to know my brothers better, to put the Ph.D. I'd worked so hard to achieve into action. Now that I knew what it felt like to *be* a volcano, I thought adding my unique perspective to the scientific community might also do some good.

Like I'd said to Gael, being able to spend the day in my world and the nights in this one made sense on every level. We'd just have to see if I could make that happen.

FORTY

CONLEY

"ARE YOU SURE?" I asked Kyle as we began our journey back to Dóiteán. It'd been over two months since we'd had an active eruption at our mountain.

"I'm sure I want to try. I'm also sure you need to go see your family."

"I know," I said, pouting. "But it's not like I don't see them all the time in my dream state, what's the difference?"

"Not sure, but you're doing this for me," Kyle said. "Because, you love me, right?"

"Yes, I do love you, Kyle Franklyn. With all my heart, I do."

The year I'd spent with Kyle waiting for our mountain to calm down had been amazing, remarkable, everything I'd ever wanted, and so much more. We'd become friends with the dragons, and as Kyle said, even like family.

Dubh had taken me under his wing, quite literally, showing me how to be a dragon, including how to fly.

Sometimes Kyle joined us, but not as often as I wanted. I'd transform into a dragon and stay that way for the rest of my life if it were up to me. Well, except I didn't want to lose Kyle. I liked our life together too.

And in the dream state, which I was surprisingly good at creating, I could visit my parents and grandmother with no difficulty. Even Mr. Cho and I had spent some time together.

But Kyle was right. It was different from visiting in person, at least with my family. With him, it was the same whether we were in our dream state or physically... well, *physical* wasn't exactly right. We weren't really what you'd call physical beings any longer.

When the volcano erupted, we physically became our mountain, just like the dragons. But, we also had a form outside of the mountain. Of course, that was why we couldn't be around people while erupting. We were still an embodiment of the mountain itself. Even in spiritual form, we'd be dangerous to be around, something Kyle would have to keep in mind if he was able to live among people.

He was convinced our volcano would go quiet, then extinct, after it finished erupting. "That's how cinder cone volcanoes work. We released the pressure from the other volcanoes. Now we'll just go back to sleep," he'd explained.

I didn't feel that was our destiny. I felt the wild energy of the lava flowing inside me. I knew he did as well, but I thought he needed to believe he could lead a normal life outside our volcanic existence.

We spent a few days with my parents. Chemeketa and Dóiteán had created a new kind of alliance, where people could come and go freely through the portal. Both sides had built protections that required some knowledge of how the energies worked and some ability to work that energy for all who crossed.

That was to ensure the two dimensions were safe-guarded against the wrong people coming through.

Chemeketa's laws about silence were more about pro-tecting against exploitation, especially now that both Chemeketa and Dóiteán were powerful in their own right. Not to mention Dóiteán was now protected by me and the other dragons. No one in their right mind would come through the portal who wished to harm our village.

Chemeketa needed our fire energy. The population had grown old, and the people from Dóiteán could help breathe life back into the community. The battle against the darkness had shown us that we'd lost something by not having the other elements represented. So, it was a good compromise that the portal became more accessible.

Not only that, but there were so many people from that side of the portal who desired a simpler life. Dóiteán, although still a modern place, provided that. Already the village had expanded, adding over twen-ty-five new families. Even my dad, who was pretty set in his ways, admitted he liked how things were going.

He was growing older too, which was why I thought he finally decided to start holding those elections for the village leadership. Well, that and he was ready to retire. And since I was now one of the dragons the community had been built to protect, it was clear I was never going to take that position. Of course, I made a point to fly over the village with Dubh from time to time, just to drive that point home a little harder.

"Can you two meet with us before Kyle crosses over?" Mr. Cho asked.

We both nodded and followed him into my parents' formal sitting room. "I'm sure you know the darkness was defeated, but we don't think it's completely gone," Mr. Cho said.

"Yes, I've spoken to my brothers about it. It should've been defeated when Conley and I overcame it, and we're confused why it wasn't," Kyle said.

"In a way, you did. The actual curse that your father cast no longer has power, but his curse became more when it partnered with the chaos here in our dimension," my grandmother said.

She took a deep breath, then drank a sip of her tea before continuing. "You must remember, there must always be balance. There are four elements, son, not three," she explained, then looked at Kyle. "Somehow, your father was connected to another person. It could be a nephew, cousin... I'm unsure who it is, but another man's energy will also have some impact on the darkness that remains."

"How do you know this?" Kyle asked.

She sighed. "I'm a seer," she said. "I've never been very good at moving fire energy, not like the others here, but I've always had a gift with divination. I've spent a great deal of time trying to figure out why the darkness hasn't subsided, and lately, I feel a presence. Someone connected to you. I've been unable to ascertain more than that, but I think you are doing right by returning to your dimension. I believe he will come to you, to Chemeketa. If he does, you must help him fight the final fight against what's left of your father's darkness."

Kyle frowned. "I'll speak to my brothers, and maybe see if we can do some research on our side. I... I no longer feel my grandma."

My own grandmother shook her head. "No, she's... transitioned." She looked perplexed for a moment. "Well, she has mostly transitioned. There's still a connection to this side of the veil, but it's complicated."

Kyle sighed. "Thank you, Mohini," he said.

The rest of the evening was spent with my family. Mostly it was them embarrassing me about things that had happened throughout my childhood.

The next day I walked with Kyle back to the portal. There was no fear that he'd be attacked since we were stronger than any darkness now. The only threat we faced now was the chaos our dragon family had taught us to recognize as something that always existed within ourselves.

"You going to be okay?" Kyle asked as the tears slipped from my eyes.

"I'm sorry, yeah... I'm..."

Kyle pulled me into an embrace and let me cry on his shoulder. "Sweetheart, I'm here," he said, putting his hand over my heart. "I'll see you tonight when we both sleep."

"I know, but it still feels like you're going away."

Kyle kissed me deeply, then took my hand and placed it over his heart. Instantly, the matching ruby tattoos on our chests began to glow. "Neither of us is ever alone. If you need me, you just have to call me, and I'll do the same. We are part of each other, literally, okay?"

I nodded. "Yeah, I know."

We kissed for several moments before Kyle turned from me and walked into the cave that held the portal.

I waited to see if he went through without any problems, and I felt it when he crossed. Kyle had gone, but like he said, we were never really apart. We were each a part of the other, be it in our hearts or the volcano we'd poured ourselves into creating, and that would never change.

I turned then and called upon Dubh, letting him know I was transitioning into my dragon form. Red scales glistened in the early morning sun as I flew back to Dearg's base, and the cabin Kyle and I called home.

Forty-One

Kyle

RELIEF WASHED OVER ME as I crossed the portal and was immediately met by the leader of the Kels. "Welcome back, dragon," Edward said, causing me to smile.

"That's going to be my nickname now, isn't it?" I asked.

"Yes, I'm sure anyone who knows your story will think of you that way now."

"You felt me come through then?" I asked, confused why he was here since portal security was no longer necessary.

He laughed. "Yes, we felt the portal vibrating before you even went through it. You have to know, as an active volcano, you're quite a force to be moving through dimensions."

"Did my coming through create any problems?" I asked, concerned.

"No, we anticipated you would eventually want to come back to see your family, so with your brothers' help, we reinforced it, making it stronger. Now every time you move through, you add to that reinforcement."

"Cool, that's clever," I said as he led me down the path toward Chemeketa.

It shouldn't have surprised me that my essence was larger than I felt. I knew I was the mountain. I'd felt the volcano inside me from its inception. Even while I wandered aimlessly through the fog, I knew it was because I was becoming something different. Something more than I'd been before.

Of course, at the time, I thought I was becoming a spirit, and in a way, I guessed that was exactly what had happened. I had become the volcano... with my now fiancé.

I arrived at Drew and Lance's to a huge celebration. They had assembled our family and friends for a party. I figured it required my man to be with us and thought this was as good a time as any to see if we could bridge the two dimensions.

I excused myself and went out back to the little bench by the stream. Then, placing my hand over my heart and the ruby tattoo that existed there, I called to Conley.

I immediately saw him in my mind's eye. *Everything okay?* he asked, concerned.

"It's good. Do you want to try to come to this dimension through me? Like we discussed?" I asked. I was physically in this dimension, and would be spending most of my time with Conley in the dream state, but I wondered if he'd like to visit with me and my brothers physically.

"Sure, but are you not tired after your journey?"

"No, I'm perfectly fine. But my family are all gathered for a party. If you're willing, I'd like you to join us."

"I'm willing, and excited. Let's try."

I loved that Conley always seemed to be interested in trying new things. I grounded myself, pulling energy from the volcanic forces deep within the earth, then willed my man to be here with me. This confirmed our and the dragons' theory that as long as one of us were physically present on one side of the dimension to tether the other, we could travel in spirit form between the two.

When I opened my eyes, there he was, smiling at me. "So, are you sure this won't hurt you?" I asked, concerned maybe it was too much.

"No, Dubh said it should be fine. We're technically both tethered to our mountain. I'm also tethered to you, so since you are here, I... well, I don't know all the details, but he thinks we are fine."

I chuckled, threw my arm across the shoulder of my amazing man, and led him back to the house.

Everyone seemed excited to see him. Jennie had a hundred and one questions, which he answered with relish, especially the ones about him being a dragon and what it was like to fly. The question of whether or not she could ride him, well, that was something that would have to wait to be seen. Maybe if she could come to the meadow in a dream state, that's what I told her, at least. And maybe if her sperm daddy, as she called Lance, never found out.

"I wish we could summon your grandmother," Drew said as the night drew to a close. "We need to know why the darkness hasn't been defeated."

I'd told them what Mohini had told me, and noticed sadness cross Drew's face as I confirmed what I thought he must've already known. When I asked about the fourth person, the mystery relative of some sort who would ultimately break the curse, none of us could figure out who the man could be. Although, Drew did go to his mantel and took down the fourth box Grandma had left.

"Maybe it's time to open this," he said as he unsealed an envelope that sat under the box, and read the letter to us.

Drew,

I'm unsure who this final box belongs to. I do, however, know that it belongs to someone important. This stone is a sapphire, the symbol of water and specifically, the ocean. I didn't know what to do with it when I had my other stones formed for my grandsons, but I felt it was going to be needed. So, I had it turned into a bracelet.

My only clue to who this belongs to is a feeling I had years ago that someone was brought into this world who was connected to me in some way. I must believe it was that person who should have this stone, although I've never been certain.

Regardless, I leave this in your hands, so when the time comes for it to go to the person it belongs to, you will be able to pass it to them.

With all my love to you,

Gwen

"I'll say it again, I think it's time for us to find Dad," Crea said.

Lance sighed deeply. "I already found him. He's living in a nursing facility outside Portland. I'll make arrangements for us to visit him, but we shouldn't have expectations that he can communicate with us. The investigator I used to help me find him said he's suffered a stroke and is, for the most part, incapacitated."

We all sat in silence for a moment, digesting the news. "Then let's plan to go soon," I said. "Conley and I are trying this life out, but it's an experiment. I'm still tied to Conley and our volcano in Dóiteán. I may not be able to stay on this side forever. Only time will tell. But, I think I'm strong enough to last a while."

"I'll make the call tomorrow," Lance said.

With that, we all went to our rooms. Well, except for Conley and me. We walked back to the stream, and I asked him how he felt. "It's good. I feel strong here. I'm guessing anywhere you are, I'll feel strong," he said.

"Tonight, I look forward to seeing you back at our home. Do you think it'll work?" I asked.

He shrugged. "Probably, especially with Dearg working her magic to help build the connection. You know that dragon is all about love."

I chuckled. "Too much. Between her and my grandmother, it's been intense."

He smiled. "Okay, go to bed. If all goes to plan, I'll see you in our dreams."

I kissed him tenderly and placed my hand over his tattooed heart while he placed his over mine.

As we kissed, I closed my eyes. When I opened them he was gone, and my heart felt a level of loneliness I'd never known. *Gods, I hope this dream state thing works*, I thought and went into Drew and Lance's house to go to sleep and find out.

After a fantastic night with my fiancé, I woke up refreshed and ready for the day. Not for the first time I was extremely thankful the body was able to rest while the mind was busy in its dream state. My brothers and I ended up driving to our father's nursing home and were immediately led into his room.

His eyes were closed, and he appeared to be asleep. "He isn't able to speak and rarely wakes up," the nurse had told us.

"Do you think we should attempt to speak to him?" I asked as the three of us stood around the bed.

Lance nodded, closed the door, and passed around three bottles of water.

"This has Grandma's potion in it. Drew and I used it to keep the darkness at bay. I'm assuming the cantation is still around, and it's best we're prepared in case anything comes at us."

We all took a drink of the water. The taste made me smile, as it reminded me of the tea Grandma drank all the time when we were kids.

"Okay, join hands," Lance said.

He began chanting the same words over and over.

"Father of ours, let us in."

Both Crea and I joined in, and within seconds we were hit by a familiar darkness. Luckily, it was very weak, unable to do anything other than feel menacing. We pushed our way through it, and there stood our father. Even in the trance, he seemed frail.

"Father, we have come to speak with you," Lance said, and I could hear the anger in his voice. *"We have each defeated your curse and the cantation that pursued us, but the darkness persists. Why does it remain?"*

Our father shook his head. Apparently, he was unable to respond, but he waved his hand weakly over his head, and visions began to appear between him and us. A little tow-headed boy ran around a room and into his mother's arms. He was laughing until our father tried to take him from her.

When the boy shrieked, I instantly knew he was our brother. A fourth brother, a half-brother. Was he was plagued by the same damned curse?

"Where is he?" Crea demanded, and when I turned toward him, a tear had slid down his face.

Our father shrugged and the vision changed to an argument between him and the boy's mother. We couldn't hear what she said, but it was clear she was kicking him out. The boy, maybe five at that point in his life, stood solemnly watching them argue. I could see the resolve in his expression. He disliked our father as much as we had.

The vision cleared then, and the world went black. When I opened my eyes, our father was breathing hard. Lance sighed and opened the door for us to leave.

He and Crea left, but I stayed at the foot of Dad's bed. "Why?" I asked. "Why did you do that to us? How could you send something so dark, so..."

Tears slipped out of my eyes, and I felt a hand on my shoulder. I felt the energy around me shift, and knew I'd somehow reached out to Conley in my sadness. I turned to see him standing next to me. "I don't understand how he could do that to us, and now to find out he had another kid? I have another brother, Conley."

My fiancé put his arm around me and pulled me into a hug. "Shh, it'll be okay," he said.

"No, what he did will never, *ever* be okay."

Conley kissed me before he disappeared. Looking back one last time at the man who'd done so much to hurt our family, I shook my head. "I will never understand why you cursed us, but I survived. We all did, Dad. We survived your hatred."

I joined my brothers at the entrance of the care home, and the three of us walked out together, now clear on who would inherit the fourth stone. I was not sure if that made me more or less upset, but there would be time to deal with complicated feelings later. All I knew was we had another brother out there somewhere who needed us and didn't even know it. Now we just had to find him.

NEXT

The series ends with:
Sapphire Water-Book Four of the Witch Brothers Saga

Available at your favorite bookseller

Join Blake's email list to get advance notice of new books and receive his occasional newsletter:

www.blakeallwood.com

MM Romance
By Blake Allwood

Transitions Series
Aiden Inspired
Suzie Empowered (MF Romance)
Bobby Transformed

Chance Series
Love By Chance
Another Chance With Love
Taking A Chance For Love

Romantic Series
Romantic Renovations (1)
Romantic Rescue (2)
Romantic Recon (3)

Melody Series
Melody of the Heart
Melody of the Snow

Road to Rocktoberfest Anthology
Changing His Tune - 2022

Coming Home Series (2023)
A Long Way Home
Family Home
Down Home
…and many more

Novellas
Tenacious
Moon's Place

Romantic Fantasy
By Adam J. Ridley

Big Bend Series
Love's Legacy (1)
Love's Heirloom (2)
Love's Bequest (3)

The Witch Brothers Series
Emerald Earth
Diamond Air
Ruby Fire
Sapphire Water

Blake Allwood was born in west Tennessee, then moved to Kansas City MO after earning a degree in Early Childhood Education from Graceland College in Lamoni, Iowa. He met his husband Shaun in 1995 and they officially married in 2015, once gay marriage was legalized; although they still consider Valentines Day 1995 as their true "anniversary date". Twenty-two years later (2017), after fostering 12 children together, he and his husband sold their home, purchased an RV and began traveling the country with their two dogs.

Typically, Blake can be found relaxing in the RV or by the fire with his laptop and their Jack Russell Terrier, Buddy, curled up between his legs demanding attention. Denver, their Siberian Husky mix is often asleep at his feet or playing tug of war with Blake's husband.

Most of Blake's stories are inspired by the places they have visited in their ongoing travels. His first book, *Aiden Inspired*, was released in 2019 and he has now written over 20 books. In 2023 he is releasing the *Coming Home* series which is comprised of ten-plus sweet contemporary romance novels that are based on a fictional town in his home state of Tennessee.

Blake also writes under the pen name of Adam J. Ridley for his urban fantasy fans looking for stories revolving around gay characters. His first series is The Witch Brothers Saga, starting with ***Emerald Earth***.

BIBLIOPRIDE.COM

BOOKS BY LGBTQ+ AUTHORS

www.bibliopride.com

www.ingramcontent.com/pod-product-compliance
Lightning Source LLC
Chambersburg PA
CBHW061545210726
48287CB00006B/2078